CAUSE OF DEATH

When Mrs. Sophie Easterberg was found dead on her bedroom floor in the picturesque village of Five Meadows, it was apparent that she had been murdered. The obvious suspect was Dave Lucas, an ex-Borstal boy recently in her employ, who had since disappeared, and the village wasted little time in attributing the crime to him.

Detective Superintendent Manton of the Yard was despatched to take charge of the case, and he soon ran Lucas to earth. But was he guilty? And, even if he was, would a jury convict him?

Other titles in the Black Dagger Crime series:

Spy in Chancery by Kenneth Benton
A Coffin from the Past by Gwendoline Butler
A Delivery of Furies by Victor Canning
Murder Is for Keeps by Peter Chambers
Three Days' Terror by John Creasey
And So To Murder by Carter Dickson
Death Is a Red Rose by Dorothy Eden
The March Hare Murders by Elizabeth Ferrars
Death Has Deep Roots by Michael Gilbert
Death of an Alderman by John Buxton Hilton
The So Blue Marble by Dorothy B. Hughes
Gently Go Man by Alan Hunter
The Blood Running Cold by Jonathan Ross
Deadline by Martin Russell
Harbingers of Fear by Dorothy Simpson
The End of the Web by George Sims

FOREWORD

MICHAEL UNDERWOOD is a writer in the classic tradition of British crime writers: easy, urbane, and professional in the best possible sense. You pick up an Underwood story in the comfortable knowledge that you are in safe hands.

The distinguishing feature of any Underwood detective story is the gripping trial scene, but then Michael Underwood is the pseudonym of a lawyer and he knows what he is writing about. *Cause of Death* features two splendid trial sequences: one in a Magistrates' Court and the second in the Old Bailey itself.

Barristers, with solicitors and their clerks, walk with conviction through an Underwood book, helping to untangle the plot. But they are not only representatives of the legal system, nor are they always the investigators – in *Death in Camera* a judge is murdered.

So, one way and another, lawyers play an active part in the development of an Underwood plot, just as they did in the books of Cyril Hare and still do in the thrillers of Michael Gilbert, with both of whom Michael Underwood bears comparison. This seems a more accurate parallel than that frequently drawn with the American Erle Stanley Gardner, creator of the flamboyant Perry Mason.

In *Cause of Death* the crime is investigated in the orthodox way by a policeman, Detective Superintendent Manton, but in the background there is Paul Steadman, a lawyer working in the office of the Director of Public Prosecutions. In some later books the main detective work which unwinds the plot is carried out by a lawyer, a young woman named Rosa Epton.

It may also be the author's legal training that helps him to see each side of a case, and in his books we notice the sensitive, even merciful handling of the murderer. One of the strengths of *Cause of Death* is the sympathetic treatment of the young offender, Dave Lucas, who may or may not be a murderer. The people who walk through his plots are, in the main, intelligent people from a middle class world, of the sort who will not usually expect to come the way of murder.

But Michael Underwood also shows sympathy for those, like Dave Lucas, from a less privileged stratum.

Since Michael Underwood started writing in 1954, he has produced some thirty or more novels, all of a consistently high standard. He writes with a simplicity and a kind of candour that is spiced with flashes of sharpness and humour. He excels in realistic, believable plots in which the identity of the murderer, although well hidden, is totally credible when revealed. There are no slippery tricks or cheating in an Underwood plot. The attentive reader, alert for the clues, can deduce who the murderer is. The motive for the crime is similarly convincing. In *Cause of Death* it might be said to be personal survival. But what makes us believe in this particular murderer is that the killing is opportunist. Underwood knows that, of all crimes, murder is very often the least premeditated. He understands that for many murderers it is a terrible, spur of the minute act into which they are pushed by emotions beyond control.

Michael Underwood knows the anatomy of a murder and lets the reader see it clearly. In his quiet way, he is a very serious writer.

GWENDOLINE BUTLER

THE BLACK DAGGER CRIME SERIES

The Black Dagger Crime series is a result of a joint effort between Chivers Press and a sub-committee of the Crime Writers' Association, consisting of Marian Babson, Peter Chambers and chaired by John Kennedy Melling. It is designed to select outstanding examples of every type of detective story, drawing on the early works of CWA members, so that enthusiasts will have the opportunity to read once more classics that have been scarce for years, while introducing them to a new generation who have not previously had the chance to enjoy them.

ONE

PAUL STEADMAN disliked London's pigeons and everything about them: in particular their beady-eyed complacency and the fussy, conceited struttings of the courting males. It seemed to Steadman that there was not an hour of the day nor a season of the year when, from his office window, he could not see a harassed female bird being relentlessly stalked by an ardent suitor. From his room, which was at the rear of the Director of Public Prosecutions' building, he had an unrivalled view of chimneypot scenery; and always the pigeons.

Steadman looked up from the file of papers before him and yawned. He reckoned it would take him another half an hour to finish reading them, and though there was no compulsive need for him to stay on this evening and do so, he decided that he might as well. Except for fraud cases, which were too indigestible and usually too bulky, he always liked to have a straight read through of his papers. Even if he did not retain very much, he at least knew what was there. It was the principle of turning over all the stones for a quick look before making a closer examination of what each revealed.

The door of his room opened and Tom Coles came in.

'Hello, Paul, still at it?'

'Mm-mm, thought I'd just finish reading this lot.'

Coles cocked his head on one side. He was a short, square-shouldered man with startling red hair and the engaging air of a dog determined to please.

'What is it? Another bloody fraud? That seems to be my diet these days.'

'No, it's a murder. Chap killed his wife because she kept boiling his eggs too hard.'

'Sounds reasonable. How'd he do it?'

'Oh, with the usual chopper.'

Coles nodded understandingly.

'If it's not a chopper, it's a poker or a hammer . . .'

'Or a tie or a pyjama cord', Steadman added with a faint smile.

'I know. Can't think of a room in my house that doesn't contain at least half a dozen lethal instruments.'

'The lavatory?' Steadman asked laconically.

'Disinfectant. Poisonous as hell. Anyway, where did this happen?'

Paul Steadman told him and echoed the groan that followed.

'Lousy dump of a place.'

'Possibly that's why people commit murders there.'

Coles looked round for an ashtray. He knew there wasn't one and that Steadman, a non-smoker, declined to pander to the needs of his visitors, but he always felt obliged to remark on the deficiency. 'Oh, of course, you haven't got one', he said with a reproachful sigh. He walked to the window and stubbed his cigarette on the ledge outside. Steadman watched him with a tolerant smile. Turning back, Coles went on, 'Talking of which, I see there's been one down at Five Meadows.'

'A murder?'

'Yep, capital murder too, by the sound of it. An old girl found with her head bashed in and a lot of stuff stolen. The Chief Constable's called in the Yard.'

'Where did you hear all this?'

'Well, there was quite a piece in this morning's paper

about the old lady's body being found on her bedroom floor, and then there was a small paragraph at midday about the Yard being called in. Don't you read newspapers, Paul?' he asked, with mock incredulity.

'Usually, but not this morning. Jane overslept and I had a fearful rush to get here at all.'

'What do you mean, *Jane* overslept, what were *you* doing?'

'Oversleeping too.'

Tom Coles sighed. 'There's no danger of that when you have five brawling brats in the house. How is Jane, by the way?'

'Fine, thanks, Tom. She's been bitten by a writing bug and spends most of her time sucking her pencil and staring pensively at a blank sheet of paper.'

'What's she writing? A thriller based on one of your cases?'

'No, children's stories. She's certain there's a gold mine in it, but so far hasn't discovered where.' Abruptly he said, 'A girl she knew at school and vaguely keeps up with lives at Five Meadows.'

'The old lady who was murdered was seventy-four. Doesn't sound like a school chum of Jane's.'

There was a silence as Coles stared out of the window and Paul Steadman mentally measured the number of pages he had still to read.

'Well, I think I'll say good night, Paul if I can't lure you away yet. Shan't see you tomorrow. I'm in court: rape at Rugby.'

' 'Night, Tom', Steadman called after him as Coles bustled out.

Steadman passed a hand through his hair and bent once more over the papers on his desk. It was several minutes, however, before he could muster his concentration again.

He sat staring at the print with a small contented smile, thinking of Jane, his wife. She was only a year younger than himself; they'd both been over thirty when they had married seven years before. Jane, who was small and snug and ever full of enthusiasm for some new interest, bless her! And how glad he was of this, seeing that they hadn't any children. *He* hadn't minded so much, and now Jane too had got over the bitterness and disappointment. He turned his head and gazed at his profile reflected in the window, the Roman nose, the dark brown hair greying at the temples (supposedly so distinguished) but not yet thinning, and the quiet, observant eyes. He jutted out his chin and fingered beneath. Time, he decided, to go on another of his half-hearted diets. Reluctantly, he forced his attention back to his papers.

By the time he had finished, he was pondering, as so often he began to when reading murder cases, the hidden dark recesses of the human mind. A woman boiled her husband's eggs too hard and was killed. His own wife's Aunt Delia, though convinced she had a small bird lodged in her left breast, walked the streets in freedom. The one would be living out his days in an institution for criminal lunatics; the other would continue to be fussed over and humoured by a cook, a parlourmaid and a stream of visiting nieces. Which was the madder? But who knew when Aunt Delia might not suddenly seize a knife and slit herself open to release the bird! And supposing instead she slit open the cook for forgetting to order its seed, then Aunt Delia too would end up in Broadmoor. Life with the mentally unbalanced was wholly unpredictable, and the psychiatrists usually arrived on the scene too late.

On his way home, Paul Steadman bought an evening paper. The murder at Five Meadows had by now assumed front page importance. The report which he read came under the headline, 'WEALTHY WIDOW BATTERED'. It ran:

'Seventy-four year old Mrs. Sophie Easterberg, a well-known resident of the picturesque village of Five Meadows, was yesterday evening found murdered in the bedroom of her mansion home which stands outside the village, only twenty miles from London. She had been battered to death and the police believe that the motive was robbery. Her body was discovered about five o'clock when her nephew, Captain Richard Corby, called at the house to see her. It is thought she had been dead some hours and lain slain in the empty house till found. The Chief Constable today called in Scotland Yard and Detective Superintendent Manton and Detective Sergeant Yates of the murder squad arrived in the village shortly before noon. The police are working on the theory that the murderer knew that Mrs. Easterberg's companion, Miss Violet Chatt, had the day off each Wednesday and that Mrs. Easterberg would therefore be alone in her mansion.'

There followed further speculation about the crime which Steadman did not bother to read. As it was, he was prepared for Mrs. Easterberg not to have been wealthy, for her mansion to be a modern villa and for her body to have been found in the kitchen, not the bedroom. A close acquaintanceship with criminal cases had taught him to be sceptical of most press items about them. The more authentic they sounded, the more sceptical he became. All he felt justified in accepting was that a Mrs. Easterberg of Five Meadows had died a violent death.

With the paper tucked under his arm, he turned into his own gate, paused to gaze with proprietorial pride at the patch of front garden which he assiduously tended each week-end, and entered his home.

It was a small but pleasant house in an agreeable

modern suburb which catered for the middle-range professional and executive classes. For most of these it was just another staging area on their way to the top, but for Paul and Jane Steadman, who didn't contemplate anything grander, it was home.

Steadman threw his hat down on the functional hall chair and sang out his wife's name.

'Ja-ane.'

'Here, sweetheart', she replied, from the living-room. Her tone sounded preoccupied. Steadman entered the room and saw the reason.

'Muse in good form?' he asked, walking over to where she sat scribbling in a notebook on her knee.

'Mmm, just let me finish this sentence.'

Steadman watched her with an affectionate smile; the pink tip of her tongue protruded between her lips while she wrote.

'If this story doesn't sell, I give up', she said, as she laid pencil and notebook on the floor beside her and leapt up to give her husband a hug. 'It's a darling one.'

'All about fairies?'

'Children don't go in for fairies these days', she replied briskly. 'They're completely outmoded. Went out with button boots. No, this story's all about Stanley, the Spider, and how he stows away in a moon rocket to visit Moolie.'

'Moolie?'

'Yes, she's the nearest thing they have to a spider on the moon. She has no legs but is fitted with eight tiny skis instead, and she can only see out of the top of her head which means . . .' Paul Steadman sat down and let his wife exhaust her pent-up enthusiasm for Moolie. Then, handing her the evening paper, he said:

'Isn't Five Meadows where that friend of yours lives? That girl you were at school with?'

'Linda Corby, do you mean? Why, what's happened there?'

'An old lady's been murdered. It says her body was discovered by her nephew, Richard Corby.'

'That's Linda's husband. He grows tomatoes', Jane added inconsequentially. 'And other things, of course. Cucumbers and lettuce.'

'Does he have an aunt?'

'Does he not! Aunt Sophie. Linda's always on about her. At least, that is on the odd occasions we meet or she rings up. Then I get a long moan about what Aunt Sophie's done or not done, and how difficult she is. Of course, poor Linda's a bit tiresome herself in many ways and I think Aunt Sophie used to give her a real inferiority complex. But how awful for them! Murdered! Linda's sure to ring me up about it; I'm her sympathetic friend.' She paused and then asked eagerly, 'Are you likely to do the case, darling?'

Her husband's tone was mildly reproving. 'Nobody's been arrested or charged yet.'

TWO

DETECTIVE SUPERINTENDENT MANTON and Detective Sergeant Yates had, as the papers stated, arrived in Five Meadows shortly before noon, which was approximately one hour after they had been sent for by the Assistant Commissioner (Crime) and told to be on their way.

How Five Meadows had managed to remain utterly unspoilt at a time when London's suburban growth had been as remorseless as a tide of creeping lava was something of a miracle. A part explanation lay in the fact of its not being on the railway and also sufficiently far off a main road to have been unnoticed by the hurrying throngs. Moreover, it is surrounded by low-lying meadows which are invariably waterlogged several months each year, and which have made it unsuitable for expansion. Speculative builders had taken one look and sought elsewhere to plough in their profits.

When Manton and Yates arrived at the local police station, their steps were directed on to Five Meadows Chase, Mrs. Easterberg's house, by the village constable's wife.

'You'll find them all up there, sir', she said.

Five Meadows Chase, they discovered, lay on the eastern outskirts of the village, the entrance being about three hundred yards past the last cottage. The house itself was at this point hidden by a beech coppice and first sight of it came shortly after they had turned up the drive. A wide apron of green lawn came into view and beyond a giant cedar which stood guard along one edge could be seen the white, sun-washed walls of a low rambling house.

As they pulled up outside the front door, a man emerged and came over to them.

'Superintendent Manton?' He didn't wait for a reply and went on, 'I'm Detective Sergeant Spruille, sir. I'm sorry there wasn't anyone down at the local station to guide you here, but we're a bit pushed for men when a job like this breaks. Detective Superintendent Blaker is up in the bedroom, waiting for you.'

Blaker, whom Manton knew well, was the head of the county C.I.D.

The two Yard officers followed Sergeant Spruille into the house and upstairs.

At first glance, it was just the sort of house that Manton would have expected a comfortably-off old lady to live in. Everything had an air of permanence. There was a profusion of furniture and the walls were hung with hunting-prints. A fine old grandfather clock stood at the foot of the stairs, whose carpet was now wearing thin. The slight hint of shabbiness did nothing to diminish the impression of lived-in comfort.

The room to which Sergeant Spruille led them was the middle one of three.

'Mr. Manton and Sergeant Yates are here, sir', he announced as he opened the door.

'Hello, Manton', the county C.I.D. man said. 'Apart from moving the body, we've left everything just as it was found.' He was a big, bluff man who wasted no time on greetings or comments about the weather. Though he was not proposing to admit it, he was not sorry that his Chief Constable had decided to enlist Scotland Yard's aid. Not long ago he had had a big murder inquiry on his hands which had got nowhere, when everything had seemed to be in his favour too. This time someone else could carry the can.

A huge mahogany double bed covered by a pink spread was the dominating feature of Mrs. Easterberg's bedroom. Between the two windows with their faded chintz curtains stood a dressing-table, and against the near wall a tall chest of drawers. There was a chintz-covered armchair; and a heavy wardrobe stood at the far side of the room.

Manton noticed that one of the dressing-table drawers was open and that its contents appeared in disorder. An open handbag protruded.

Superintendent Blaker said:

'That wallet on the floor'—he nodded at an Italian leather notecase lying just beneath the dressing-table—'that came from her handbag. It's empty now. According to the companion, there'd have been fifteen to twenty quid in it.' He went on, and Manton thought he detected a slight note of malice in his tone, 'But don't get excited, we've tested it for fingerprints and there bain't none.'

On the floor close to where they were standing and not far from the door lay a number of articles that might have been put there as part of a test in deduction. A heavy china vase rested on its side against the corner of the chest of drawers. Over the pink carpet were scattered bits of pampas grass, the feathery fragments lying like chaff. Nearby lay a soft cushion and beside that a poker.

'Is that what she was killed with?' Manton asked, nodding at the poker.

'Yes and no. It's undoubtedly what she was hit over the head with. It's got blood and hairs on it, which presumably came from the old lady, though lab examination will tell for certain. But just before you arrived, Dr. Innes was on the phone and he's pretty certain that the cause of death was suffocation.'

Manton looked down at the cushion at his feet.

'How was she found?'

'Lying face downwards in that cushion.'

'Incidentally, who did find her?'

'Her nephew, a man named Corby. He and his wife live in a cottage at the other end of the village. He came up to visit his aunt just after five o'clock yesterday evening and found her dead.'

'When does Dr. Innes think she died?'

'He thought it was between twelve and sixteen hours before he first saw the body, which was about midnight. Incidentally, we had a helluva job finding him. Phoned up one ruddy place after another. Eventually ran him to earth at a theatre. We didn't move the body to the mortuary till after he'd got here. He did half his p.m. then and came back this morning to finish it off.'

Manton nodded. 'Oh, well, I suppose it doesn't make much difference, it's murder whichever way you look at it. Same as if you deliberately threaten someone with a knife till they walk backwards out of a window and die of a busted head.' He paused and said reflectively, 'Wonder how the cushion came to be on the floor, though.'

'Could have got there in the course of a struggle', Blaker remarked. 'There obviously was one; this vase getting knocked over, for example. Or, and I think this is much more likely, the burglar was surprised by the old girl coming into the room; he lost his head and attacked her with the poker, probably only intending to knock her senseless, and then before he fled, he stuck the cushion under her head, hoping it might save her life and save him from a charge of capital murder. Because this monkey's going to swing all right when we've got him, that's quite certain.'

Manton said nothing but let his gaze roam round the room. He noticed some scratch marks over on the farther window-sill and went across to investigate. Superintendent Blaker followed him and said, 'We've photographed those, as we have everything else in the room. In my view they were made by his shoes when he climbed out.'

'You think he left by the window?' Manton asked in some surprise.

'I'm darned certain he did. We found a fine shoe-print in the flower-bed below. A deep one, as you'd expect to find if someone had jumped out. That too has been photographed and I've also had a cast made of it. Don't think you'll find any stones left unturned so far.'

'I'm sure not', Manton replied, with a faint smile. He opened the window and leant out. It was no more than an eight-foot drop if someone held on to the window ledge and let himself dangle. The bed was of soft earth and a small area of flowers had been trampled down. Five red tulips lay massacred in their stately prime. Turning back into the room he said, 'I take it there are no fingerprints anywhere?'

'No. We've examined every possible surface, but there's not one. The monkey obviously wore gloves.'

'What did the household consist of?'

'The old girl and her companion, Miss Chatt. They were the only two who lived in. Then there were various women from the village who used to come in daily to cook and clean, and there was a gardener. Mrs. Easterberg employed a good deal of local labour and was usually ready to find a job for anyone in difficulty. The village people liked her, I gather. She was apparently more ready to do things for them than for her own sort. I've got men doing a house-to-house call now, by the way. They may pick up something useful.'

Manton nodded in approval. He felt that for the time being there was little more he could learn from the bedroom.

'Where do we find the companion?' he asked.

'When I last saw her just before you arrived, she was in the kitchen brewing tea for my slaves. Want to see her?'

'I think it'd be a good idea. Where's the best place?'

'I'll get her brought along to the drawing-room. She's one of those typical middle-aged companions old ladies get hold of.' At the thought of her, Superintendent Blaker chuckled. 'Drives a vintage baby Austin too. Straight out of a book she is.'

THREE

MISS CHATT refilled the big kettle and put it back on the gas stove. She was used to making tea; only its consumers happened to be different on this occasion. The kitchen door opened and Sergeant Spruille's head popped round.

'Mind coming along to the drawing-room, Miss Chatt, the Scotland Yard officers are here now and would like to have a word with you.'

The drawing-room to which Superintendent Blaker led Manton and Yates was immediately beneath the bedroom, but was double its size. From its wide french windows there was a delightful view across buttercup meadows to the village about a mile away, which in the sunlight had the appearance of a neat model. A landscape artist could hardly have failed to set up his easel.

The room itself contained two large sofas and a number of armchairs, all covered with some thick bluey-green material. On one of the chairs a large black cat lay curled up asleep. Against three of the walls were china cabinets crammed with bric-a-brac. Any pretence at selective display had long since been abandoned.

Miss Chatt came into the room, wearing the flowered pinafore that she had come to regard as her uniform. She was a woman in the mid-forties with neat grey hair which had been recently permed. She showed no signs of being upset but nodded quietly at the officers. Then catching sight of the cat, she walked across the room, exclaiming:

'Naughty Boot! You know quite well that's not your chair. Now be off with you.' As she spoke she put a hand beneath the animal and levered it out of the chair. It arched its back in mute disdain and went over to sit in front of the french window and stare out. 'It would never have sat on that chair when Mrs. Easterberg was alive', Miss Chatt explained. 'It's really quite remarkable, isn't it, the way animals can tell that something's happened. That's his chair there, the one with the cushion on it', she went on, indicating one over by the other window. She gave a short, nervous laugh. 'But I don't suppose you want to talk about the cat.'

Manton accepted the cue and said:

'Shall we sit down, Miss Chatt? I gather that you were the last person to see Mrs. Easterberg alive yesterday. About what time would that have been?'

'Well, I always leave the house about half-past nine on my day off, that is Wednesdays, and usually I have a word with Mrs. Easterberg just before I go. To make sure everything's all right, you know, and that she has everything she needs.'

'And you did that yesterday?'

'Yes. She was in here sitting at her desk writing out a cheque. She hardly looked up when I told her I was off.'

'And when you went was she then alone in the house?'

'Yesterday she was. Normally either Mrs. Winters or Mrs. Scarlon would have been here to get her lunch and see to things. But Mrs. Winters, she's the one who does most of the cooking, is on her holiday and Mrs. Scarlon who does the housework has been away with measles, which she caught from her little boy. She's been quite bad with it, too.'

'So who's been coping with things while these ladies have been away? You?'

'Yes, but it's not been too difficult. We've let the dust accumulate and just had simple meals.'

'Mrs. Easterberg was able to manage for herself? When you were out, I mean?'

'Oh, yes. Mind you, I offered not to take my day off last week or this, but she was most insistent that I should go.'

There was a pause and Manton said:

'Why exactly did Mrs. Easterberg need to have a companion, Miss Chatt? She sounded quite a healthy person.'

'Oh, indeed. She had excellent physique, and was a most vigorous personality too.' With an air of resigned sadness, she went on, 'But in the same way that a steel knife requires a whetstone, so Mrs. Easterberg needed a companion.' As an afterthought she added, 'And of course it wouldn't have been a very good idea for her to have lived alone in this big house at her age.' She was thoughtfully silent for a moment. 'If you had spent as much of your life tending old ladies' needs as I have, you'd know what I mean. The ones who require companions are as much a breed as we companions are ourselves.' She looked up with a wistful smile and in that moment, Manton could see all the years she had spent tending the wants of exacting, querulous and often capricious old women. Humbled, bullied, patronized and miserably paid, that was how he saw Miss Chatt's life. He hoped Mrs. Easterberg had remembered her companion when she made her will. Stifling his sentimental thoughts, he said:

'And what time did you return last night?'

'At half-past nine. I left London about eight and it takes an hour and a half in my little car. I normally drive to the station and go up by train, but yesterday I did the whole journey by car as I was going to have tea with my cousin who lives at Harrow and it made it easier to have the car with me.'

'I'm sure you won't mind supplying us with details of how you spent your day. Merely a matter of routine.'

'No, of course not. I had an appointment with the hair-dresser at twelve. I expect you'd like his name. It's a little place off Brompton Road that I always go to called Monsieur Victor's. A girl named Beryl does my hair. When I left there, I . . .'

Manton broke in quickly, 'You needn't give us all the details now, Miss Chatt. We shall be asking you to make a full written statement in due course and there'll be time then. Can you remember whether the front door was locked when you left yesterday morning?'

'Oh, no, Mrs. Easterberg would never have it locked in the daytime. She wouldn't even have bothered about it at night if I hadn't insisted. She was quite fearless about burglars and all these teddy-boy people; used to think I was silly to fuss.' Again a wistful expression passed across Miss Chatt's face. 'As a matter of fact she often thought I was silly and used to tell me so. She wasn't a very tolerant person, you know; though perhaps I shouldn't say that now she's dead.'

Manton felt he was acquiring a more than clear picture of the relationship which had existed between employer and employee.

'Who might have come up to the house after you left?' he asked.

'Well, I don't really know. Wednesday's not a day any of the tradespeople call. Mr. Pringle might have looked in. He quite often used to.'

'Who's he?'

'He runs the garage in the village. Mrs. Easterberg always used to send for him when there was a job to be done like seeing to the motor-mower or fixing the fuses. He also drove her car on the rare occasions she had it out.'

From Miss Chatt's tone Manton got the impression that she didn't care for Mr. Pringle, and didn't particularly mind him, Manton, knowing it. The sniff of disapproval when she mentioned his name was too obvious to be missed.

'Wasn't the gardener at work yesterday?' he asked.

'No, he's Mrs. Winters' husband and on holiday too.'

'So that none of the staff were here at all yesterday after you left?'

Miss Chatt nodded her agreement.

Superintendent Blaker took Manton's arm and whispered loudly, 'There used to be a lad called Lucas working here. Got the sack about ten days ago.'

Manton looked across at Miss Chatt with raised eyebrows.

'That correct?'

'Yes, David Lucas. Mrs. Easterberg dismissed him. He was only here about two months.'

'What did he do?'

'He used to clean the shoes and stoke the boiler.' As though in answer to Manton's thought, she went on, 'He had a room over the stables at the back. Mrs. Easterberg took him on as an experiment.'

'Experiment!' Manton echoed in surprise.

'He'd been in trouble and recently come out of Borstal. A cousin of Mrs. Easterberg's who works as a probation officer asked if she'd give him a job. It was felt it would do him good to get away from London and the people he was mixing with up there. He was quite a decent lad and worked well; even if you did have to be on to him most of the time.'

'Why did he get the sack?' Manton asked with interest.

'Mrs. Easterberg found him wandering about upstairs one day. She never allowed him inside the house and so she told him he'd have to go. He left the same day.'

Manton and Blaker exchanged meaning glances.

'Where's his home?'

Miss Chatt shrugged her shoulders.

'Somewhere in South London, I believe. At least that's where Mrs. Easterberg's cousin works; I don't think I ever heard his home mentioned.'

Blaker gave Sergeant Spruille a peremptory nod. 'Make a note to check on that.'

'I suppose there hasn't been time to trace Lucas?' Manton asked, turning to the county C.I.D. superintendent.

Blaker shook his head. 'Green, the constable in the village, mentioned him last night, but we haven't yet taken any steps to find him.'

'I think we should now', Manton said, lowering his voice. 'At the moment he looks like being a suspect. This was just the sort of crime that might have been committed by someone of his type. Crude, senseless and with all the signs of panic afterwards.' He turned back to Miss Chatt, who had gone over to the french window and was scratching the cat's head. 'Do you happen to know the name and address of this cousin of Mrs. Easterberg's?'

'Perhaps I can help you better there.' Manton swung round at the sound of a new voice and saw standing in the doorway a tall, thin man with fair, wispy hair and a soft blond moustache.

'Oh, this is Captain Corby, Mrs. Easterberg's nephew', Miss Chatt explained.

Corby shook hands with Manton and Yates, and said, 'Yes, my wife and I live at the other end of the village. I was Aunt Sophie's nearest relative. Terrible thing this! Think you'll catch the fellow who did it?'

'If we don't, it won't be for want of trying', Manton replied coolly. Corby struck him as the type who had hung on to his military title and cultivated a façade of authority to hide the weakness which lay beneath. Moreover he always mistrusted people with silky, blond moustaches. Unreasonable, of course, but he couldn't help it.

'We're wanting to trace a lad named Lucas who, I gather, worked for your aunt up until about ten days ago and then got the sack.'

'Yes, the young scallawag, biting the hand that fed him. Too much softness these days; not enough discipline. That's the trouble. I warned Aunt Sophie against employing him, but as usual she thought she knew best. You think it may have been he who killed her?'

'What do you mean about biting the hand that fed him?' Manton chipped in.

'Well', Corby said in a knowing tone. 'I'm pretty sure he did some pilfering while he was here. Aunt Sophie used to leave money around in numerous purses and handbags and it would have been the easiest thing on earth for him to have sneaked some. She didn't actually tell me that he had. She couldn't very well, as it would have proved me right in advising her not to employ him. But for what other purpose was he wandering about the house that time she discovered him upstairs?' He cocked his head on one side and gave the police officers a shrewdly knowing look. 'Don't you agree, Miss Chatt?'

Miss Chatt, however, appeared embarrassed at being appealed to and did no more than smile apologetically and turn back to the cat.

There was a silence, then Corby said, 'I can let you

have the address of the cousin who asked Aunt Sophie to give Lucas a job. I agree that he'll be the best person through whom to try and trace him. When my aunt sacked him he cleared right out of the village. I do know that, because I asked your fellow, Green, only two or three days ago and he told me Lucas hadn't been around since then. Incidentally, I believe he was rather gone on one of the girls in the village. Don't know her name but Green'll tell you.' With an ingratiating grin he added, 'In a village like ours, the only three people who count are the doctor, the policeman and the parson. Between them they know everything.'

Manton tapped a nail against the signet ring on his little finger and looked across at Miss Chatt with a faintly worried expression. Turning back to Corby he said, 'I'd like some time to ask you about your aunt's will.'

Miss Chatt straightened up as though a needle had been stuck into her. 'Excuse me, please, I'd quite forgotten, I've left a kettle on.' She hurried out of the room, pink with embarrassment.

Superintendent Blaker gave a loud laugh. 'That got rid of her all right. You might have said you were going to take your trousers off the way she scuttled out.'

Manton smirked.

'Do you *happen* to know the terms of your aunt's will, Captain Corby?' he asked. Corby hesitated, and Manton went on, 'We'd find out anyway when probate's granted. Not that I expect it has much relevance in this case, but it's one of the numerous routine questions we have to ask.'

'As a matter of fact, her solicitor has been on to me to-day, discussing funeral arrangements and the like, and he mentioned the will.' The subject appeared to cause Captain Corby difficulty in expressing himself. The words fell from his lips only after careful selection. 'It seems that *I* am the chief beneficiary.'

'You're her nearest relative, after all', Manton remarked. 'What's the total value of her estate?'

'Just short of eighty thousand pounds, the solicitor said. Of course, that's before death duties are paid.'

'You'll still be quite a rich man, Captain Corby.'

Corby gave a short, mocking laugh.

'Actually she's tied it all up so that I shan't be able to touch the capital.'

'It's in trust then?'

Corby nodded grimly.

'You weren't expecting anything like that?' Manton asked.

'Aunt Sophie wasn't the sort of person to go blabbing about what was in her will. I assumed she'd leave me something but I knew better than to ask.'

Manton could understand the man's pique at learning that his inheritance was untouchable. There was something particularly galling to a grown person to be treated as irresponsible with money. He, Manton, could never see why the dead should worry about how their heirs blew the proceeds. Bequests didn't have to be made, but when they were, then his view was that the beneficiary should have absolute discretion. After all, the dead wouldn't be around to know, and he was all against their trying to fetter those they left behind in this mortal coil.

'Did the solicitor mention any legacies?' he asked casually.

'She left small sums to the gardener and to the two women who've worked here for a good many years. A hundred pounds each.'

'Miss Chatt included?'

Corby shook his head. 'No, she'd only been with my aunt just under twelve months. I may say that's longer than most of the companions lasted; Aunt Sophie, I'm afraid, rather despised them. Not so much as persons but as a class, I mean.'

As he spoke, there came back to Manton's mind, Miss Chatt's expression, 'She needed a companion in the same way that a steel knife needs a whetstone'.

'Just the three legacies and the bulk of the estate to you on trust, Captain Corby. That's the sum of it, then?'

'No, there was one other legacy. She left something to a man named Bob Pringle.'

'Is that the fellow who runs the garage? Miss Chatt mentioned him just before you came.'

'That's right.' Corby looked up and, fixing Manton with a blank stare, said, 'She left him her car and ten thousand pounds.'

Manton's mind raced ahead exploring the possibilities which now suddenly loomed up. Supposing, for example, Pringle had known he was being left this large sum; supposing he was in money difficulties at this moment. There would have been motive, good and strong, to kill the old lady and obtain sooner rather than later (and heaven knows how much later it might not have been) what was coming to him. And how simple to ransack a drawer, throw an empty wallet down so that the whole thing looked like the crime of a marauding burglar. He recalled his thoughts from the warren in which they were burrowing. Too much speculation in the early stages of an investigation was bad. It was apt to give rise to preconceived notions and there was then the temptation to try and twist the facts to fit them.

He turned to Corby. 'I understand that it was you

who discovered your aunt's body. Did you come up to the house for any special reason?'

'Yes, but I've already explained all this to Sergeant Spruille.'

'That's right, sir. I obtained a short statement from Captain Corby last night.'

Manton said with a placating smile, 'This isn't trying to catch you out. It's just that I haven't yet had an opportunity of reading your statement.'

'My aunt phoned me at about nine o'clock yesterday morning and asked me to look in after tea as she had something important she wished to discuss with me. I told her I'd come along sooner if she liked, but she said no, that would be soon enough.' He smiled wryly. 'She'd never let herself be the excuse for my deserting my work.'

'Did she give you any hint what she wanted to see you about?'

'No. But her tone was the rather formal one she used to adopt when somebody was in trouble about something.'

'I see. And you came about five o'clock?'

'I did. And found her lying dead on the bedroom floor. I could tell she'd been dead for some hours. I immediately phoned Dr. Price and then the police, and waited here until they arrived.'

At this moment there was a knock on the door and Miss Chatt came in, bearing a tray of teacups.

'Perhaps not quite what you men are used to at this hour of the day, but it's freshly made.' She put the tray down on a table and turned to leave. 'I shall be upstairs in my room, if you want me.' Looking towards Corby she said, 'If you have no objection, Captain Corby, I'll stay on a few days. It'll take me a little while to make my arrangements.'

'That's quite all right, Miss Chatt. Stay as long as you wish. You won't mind being alone in the house?'

'Oh, good gracious, no!' She embraced them all in her look as she went on, 'I've worked in hospitals, you know, and one gets used to death there.'

'Poor soul', Corby said with feeling after she had closed the door behind her. 'And now I suppose she'll be looking out for another job, for another crabby old lady. What a life!'

FOUR

As they trooped out of the front door Manton paused in the drive and looked back, studying the house with the air of a prospective purchaser. It was a good solid structure, white-stuccoed and wholesome.

'Care to take a squint round the back while you're here?' Superintendent Blaker asked.

'Good idea.'

Blaker led the way along the drive which cut through a high yew hedge and kinked to the left into a large paved yard. Along one side ran the kitchen quarters of the house, with the stables running out at right angles from the far end.

'We've searched there', Blaker said casually. 'Just the usual junk. The far door on the right is where the car's kept. An old pre-war model, incidentally, so I doubt whether Bob Pringle will get much for it other than as scrap.'

'Which was the room Lucas slept in?' Manton inquired.

'One above the garage. He's left nothing in it. There's only a bed and one or two sticks of furniture up there. I should think he was probably more comfortable in Borstal.'

'Mrs. Easterberg did give him a radio for the room', Sergeant Spruille put in. 'And it was nice and warm with those pipes from the boiler.'

'I suppose so', Blaker grunted, leading them across the yard and to the walled-in kitchen garden beyond. 'And that's about all', he said, when they had spent a couple of minutes surveying the tidy rows of vegetables and the fruit trees trained against the sunny red wall.

'What's the total acreage?' Manton asked.

'About twenty or thirty including the meadows.'

'Not very difficult for anyone to reach the house without being seen', Manton observed, without comment from the others.

When they returned to the cars, Blaker excused himself by saying he must return to headquarters and attend to one or two office matters.

'I'll be over again this evening. In the meantime phone me if there's anything you need. We've fixed up for you to stay in the local pub and I think you'll be well looked after. I suggest Sergeant Spruille takes you along there now and after that you may care to have a chin-wag with our chap, Green. He'll tell you as much about the local set-up as anyone can.' He got into his car, pressed the starter, engaged reverse gear with harsh grating sounds and shouted out of the window above the noise of the frantically revving engine, 'I'll have a word with Dr. Innes and the lab people before I come back.'

Manton acknowledged the message with a flip of the hand.

'That the super's own car?' he asked Sergeant Spruille.

'Yes, sir. Always drives himself; won't use an official car unless he's forced to.'

Superintendent Blaker's furious departure could still be heard as they piled into the other car and drove off.

After a quarter of an hour at 'The White Bear' where they had a pint of ale and received the most pressing assurance from the landlord that no service would be too much trouble, they set out for the police station, which was a hundred yards further down the street.

P.C. Green had just arrived back from his morning's inquiries and was in the process of unbuttoning his tunic and loosening his boots when he saw them approach. Quickly he restored himself to order and endeavoured to dismiss from his mind the plate of steak and kidney pudding which he knew his wife had just taken out of the oven for him.

Sergeant Spruille made the introductions, and Manton and Yates shook hands with the constable. Manton's eye took in the row of medal ribbons on the breast of his tunic, which indicated service in a number of widely separated theatres of war.

'Navy?' he asked pleasantly.

'That's right, sir.' Green had the same touch of country about his voice as he had in his appearance. His face was open and frank and he looked as though he could put in a whole day in the fields without noticing it.

'Anything to report?' Sergeant Spruille asked, by way of priming him.

'Not much, no, sir. As you know, Mr. Blaker wanted me to find out, if I could, where that young Lucas has got to. I had a go at his young lady, that's Jean Gawler, last night, sir, but I'm satisfied she doesn't know his whereabouts.'

'He hasn't been in touch with her since he left here ten days ago?'

'I wouldn't say he hasn't been in touch, sir. From the way she spoke, I'm pretty sure he's written to her all right, but I still don't think she knows where he is, other than that he's in London.'

'What sort of girl is Jean?' Manton asked.

'Not a bad girl at all, sir. Quite a decent girl in fact. She's seventeen and the eldest of four. Father works for Mr. Pringle. He's a mechanic, the father.' Green thoughtfully reviewed what he'd just said and then went on,

'Lucas and the girl appear to have been genuinely fond of each other, sir. The mother confirms that. She says the girl was very upset when Lucas was dismissed by Mrs. Easterberg. Talked about running away with him, but her father soon put an end to that nonsense, and she seems to have acted quite sensible since then.'

'Was Lucas ever in any trouble during the time he was in Five Meadows?'

'None at all, sir', Green said stoutly. 'Definitely none at all. Didn't really see much of him myself. When he wasn't up at The Chase, he was at the Gawlers or taking Jean to the pictures hereabouts. We don't have 'em in Five Meadows yet, sir', he added with a grin.

And that for the time being seemed to dispose of David Lucas. He had been swallowed up, though Manton hoped that it wasn't going to be too difficult to find him. He had already had Sergeant Yates phone through to the Yard to alert the Metropolitan police to keep an eye open for him.

'Did you ever hear anything in the village, Green, to suggest that Mrs. Easterberg and her nephew, Captain Corby, didn't hit it off?'

'No, sir, not in the way you mean. Mrs. Easterberg was a determined old lady who liked to have her own way; and being wealthy too, she usually got it. I have heard it said that she thought the captain lacked character: hadn't done as well in life as he should have. But I don't think it was anything more than you might expect to find in any domineering old lady whose nephew grew tomatoes instead of being an ambassador or an admiral. The captain certainly used to visit her regular. Not his wife, though. I don't think Mrs. Easterberg liked Mrs. Corby. Mind you, she was a difficult old lady.'

'You've had trouble with her yourself?'

'No, sir, but I always felt I might have on the few

occasions I had to go and see her about something or t'other. Once she saw you couldn't be browbeaten, however, she was as good as gold.'

'Did she have any children of her own?'

'It appears never, sir. And she'd been a widow for over forty years.'

'What do you know about Bob Pringle?' Manton asked, going down the list of persons in whom he was interested.

'Ah, Bob Pringle! Now there's somebody who used to get his way with the old girl from all accounts. She used to set great store by his advice and listen to everything he'd tell her. Whenever there was anything to be done to the car or a door hinge that had to be oiled, it was always "tell Bob Pringle, I'd like him to come up". And up he'd go and do the job and then stay on and have a ripe old natter with her. She used to tell him about her family and her childhood days; was even starting to teach him about stocks and shares, so I've heard.' He noticed Manton's mildly surprised expression and explained, 'Nothing's secret in a village, sir. The women who worked up there have talked.'

'Pringle himself too, maybe.'

'Not him. He's the strong, silent type Very much keeps himself to himself.'

'What age is he?'

'Bit younger than myself. Thirty-four, thirty-three perhaps.'

'Married?'

'Yes. Got a couple of kids. Mrs. Easterberg often used to send them down presents, clothes and stuff out of her garden.'

A silence ensued in which Manton digested what he had just learnt. Then, with an air of finality, he said, 'Is there anyone else in the village we ought to know about; anyone whose relationship with Mrs. Easterberg might have had a bearing on her death?'

'Well, I suppose, sir, you ought to know about Mr. Spicer', Green replied with a slightly troubled expression. Manton sat back and waited to do so. 'He's a writer, sir; not been here very long, bought a cottage and spent no end of money having it done up and modernized before he moved in. That must have been about three months ago; about February it was. Anyway, as I say, sir, he's a writer and he hadn't been here long before an article appeared in the *Gazette*—that's the county's leading paper, sir—about life in an imaginary village. I say "imaginary", because it was called Green Hill in this article, but no one who read it had the slightest doubt that it was meant to describe life in Five Meadows. And so it did, took the whole place off to a T.'

Manton broke in. 'Was it written anonymously?'

'Oh no, sir. "By Lewis Spicer" it said in bold print. There was no question of his doing anything underhand. But the point was, sir, that in this imaginary village there was an old lady who practically ruled the place and who had everyone chasing about to supply her needs, proper old witch she was made out, until . . .' At this point Green paused significantly to continue, 'a newcomer arrives in the place and so to speak breaks the witch's spell by showing the villagers how to stand up to her.'

'And Mrs. Easterberg saw herself cast in the role of witch, I take it?'

'Exactly, sir.'

'Did she take any steps to sue Mr. Lewis Spicer?'

Green chuckled. 'Not Mrs. Easterberg, sir. That wasn't her way. She counter attacked in far more direct fashion. She let it be known that in her view Five Meadows was far better off without gentlemen like Mr. Spicer.'

'That doesn't sound very damaging.'

Green ignored the interruption and went on, 'Gentlemen whose morals, she said, were better suited to public lavatories than a country village.'

'I see', Manton said slowly. 'And what sort of morals does Mr. Lewis Spicer have?'

Green looked across at Sergeant Spruille and back to Manton. 'I have put in a report to headquarters, sir. He often has young men down at the week-ends and once he tried to get friendly with a lad in the village who was home on leave from the navy. Mind you, we've no evidence against him, but there's been a good deal of talk.'

'I see', Manton said again. 'And what was his reaction to this counterblast to his article?'

'I believe he threatened her with legal action, sir, if she repeated her remarks.'

'From what I've heard, I don't imagine Mrs. Easterberg was unduly perturbed by that.'

'Nor do I, sir, but as you can imagine, it left things a bit strained between them.'

'But hardly enough to justify murder', Manton said, rising from his chair. He stifled a yawn. 'I think I'll just take a stroll through the village. Then I'd better read through all the statements you've taken.'

Sergeant Spruille tapped the folder on his knee.

'I have them here, sir.'

'Take a look at them while I'm gone, Pete', Manton said, turning to Yates.

As he reached the door, the telephone rang and he waited while P.C. Green ambled across to answer it.

'Five Meadows police station, Constable Green speaking', he said in a heavyweight tone as he put the receiver to his ear with elaborate care. There was a pause before he went on briskly, 'Yes, sir, he's still here.' Putting his hand over the mouthpiece, he looked across at Manton. 'It's for you, sir. Superintendent Blaker on the line.'

Manton at once recognized Blaker's harsh tones and held the instrument slightly away from his ear.

'Thought you'd better hear the latest. One of my fellows has been making inquiries at the post office and has had a word with the fellow who delivered mail up at The Chase yesterday. He had, amongst other things, a registered letter for Miss Chatt so remembers the occasion quite well. He says it was the last call he made in Five Meadows and the clock in the village sub-post office said a quarter to ten when he looked in to collect out-going mail. He reckons it was five to ten minutes later that he arrived at The Chase. He rang the bell and banged on the door for several minutes but couldn't get any answer, so he had to take the registered letter away with him again.' Blaker gave an explosive cough down the line and Manton grimaced. Then he went on, 'That seems to narrow down the times fairly well, doesn't it? It means the crime must have been committed very soon after Miss Chatt left at half-past nine. Almost makes one think that the fellow was waiting for her departure before entering the house.'

'Could be. So we're looking for someone who was there between, say nine thirty-five and just before ten o'clock.'

'That's it. Everything O.K.?'

'Yes thanks.'

'Right. See you in about a couple of hours' time.'

After passing on this information to the others, Manton made his escape. He wanted a short stroll on his own to go over in his mind all he had learnt in the three hours since his arrival. For the moment there was nothing more active for him to do. He was like a general who has made his battle plan and issued his orders and must patiently await developments.

As he walked along the sunlit street, he became aware of the attention his presence was exciting. Children turned and stared with wide-eyed interest, men looked up from their gardens and leaned a while on their spades to watch him pass. From inside the tiny shops, women nudged each other and went up on tiptoe to peer at him round pyramids of canned fruit salad or between sides of frozen beef. Of one thing there was no doubt, everyone knew who he was. He couldn't help feeling that they expected more of him; to see him, for example, dart forward suddenly and pick up a cigarette butt for cold appraisal. Yes, clues, that's what they obviously expected him to be searching for. Some of the younger ones probably hoped for the more electrifying manifestations of his trade. Squad cars with screeching tyres and two-way radio going down the main street at eighty miles at hour.

In a short time he had left the few shops behind him and on his left across the dappled meadows he could see The Chase, gleaming white against the luxuriant greens of nature that each spring provides. On the other side of the road was a row of thatched cottages with lovingly-tended gardens ablaze with colour. Manton paused to admire them. 'Lovely to look at but hell to live in, I guess', he murmured to himself.

Gazing down the line of cottages, he saw that a field lay between the end one and the building that came after it, which could hardly have been in greater contrast.

It was modern red-brick and yet not wholly discordant with its surroundings. It had a forecourt with two petrol pumps and a large swinging sign sticking out from the gabled roof which said 'Bob Pringle's Garage'.

Not wishing his walk to be seen as other than casual,

Manton strolled on unconcernedly until he came opposite the garage, when he paused as though toying with a sudden idea.

The front was wide open and inside he could see a farm tractor and an M.G. Magnette, the one with a wheel off, the other with the bonnet up. From out of sight came the sounds of metal working on metal. On the right of the entrance was an office with tins of car polish and various accessories displayed in the window. But there was no one there.

He stepped inside the shadow of the building and moved in the direction of the noise. Bending over a large bench against a side wall was a man with his back towards him. He was wearing a suit of surprisingly clean overalls and indeed the thing that impressed Manton above all else was the cleanliness of the place. He wouldn't have gone as far as to sit on the floor in his best suit, but it was quite unusually clean for what it was.

'Good afternoon', he called across to the man, and repeated the greeting when he didn't appear to hear. The man straightened up and looked round. His expresion was impassive as he surveyed Manton up and down.

' 'Afternoon', he answered at length.

'Are you Mr. Pringle?'

'No, but I works for him, he . . .' He halted and stared past Manton, who turned his head to follow his gaze. In the entrance stood someone who could only be the owner of the garage. He had the build of a heavyweight boxer and all the assurance that went with such a physique.

'I'm Pringle', he said. 'Want me?'

'Good afternoon, Mr. Pringle. I happened to be walking past and thought I'd look in. Nice place you've got here.' To give some meaning to his words, Manton allowed his gaze to wander round the four corners of the building.

Pringle said nothing; and indeed had not moved since Manton had become first aware of his presence. Either by nature or by intention, he was making things awkward. Manton moved towards him, and introduced himself; he felt unnecessarily, for he had no doubt that Bob Pringle, along with everyone else in the village, knew who he was. 'Could I have a word with you—in your office perhaps?'

Still without speaking Pringle turned about and walked into the small front office. Manton followed him, ostentatiously closed the door behind him and sat down on the only available chair.

'I understand you knew Mrs. Easterberg fairly well, Mr. Pringle?' Not bothering to wait for an acknowledgement of this, he went on, 'As you probably know, the police make a point of interviewing everyone who has been connected with the victim of an unsolved crime. It's part of their job. Every scrap of information they pick up is potentially important.'

While he had been speaking, Pringle had never taken his eyes off him. Now he said abruptly, 'I can't tell you anything about the murder.'

'You may not think you can, but . . .'

'I can't and that's flat.'

'But you used to go up to the house quite often and . . .'

'Only when I was sent for', Pringle broke in.

'When were you last there?'

'Last Monday; and you can check that if you want.' His tone was truculent.

Manton had no desire to get involved in sterile argument, and let the remark pass. This was a fact-finding mission, a reconnaissance, not war itself.

'How used *you* to get on with Mrs. Easterberg, Mr. Pringle?' he asked.

'All right.' Pringle looked out of the window for a

second and turning back, said, 'She treated me and the family very fairly.'

This sounded a bit of an under-statement from someone who had become the richer by ten thousand pounds in the last twenty-four hours. But perhaps he had not yet heard about his legacy. Manton decided to try and find out.

'She was pretty well off from what I hear. I suppose someone's going to benefit apart from the Exchequer.'

But Pringle merely shrugged his shoulders as though the question held no interest for him. With almost anyone else it would have been impossible for their excitement to have remained hidden if they had known of their good fortune, but in Pringle's case, Manton felt that no safe deduction could be drawn.

'Did you know this lad Lucas who used to work for Mrs. Easterberg?' he asked. Pringle nodded. 'Seen him about at all since he was sacked ten days ago?' Pringle shook his head. His whole manner was beginning to show boredom with his visitor. Manton, too, considered there was little point in remaining. He had met Pringle and seen for himself the taciturn, uncommunicative type he was. On the other hand, he could, or thought he could, understand how an old lady might have succumbed to him. Freud would probably have explained it in terms of sex. But everything could be related to sex if one was so minded. All Manton knew was that there were precedents for such things happening, for people falling under the most unlikely influences. Queen Victoria and John Brown for example.

He was about to get up when the door was thrust open and a head was poked in.

'My car ready, Bob?'

'Yes, I'll get her out for you, Mr. Spicer.'

Pringle pushed his way past Manton and disappeared

out of the office, leaving Manton and the new arrival to take stock of each other. Manton estimated Spicer to be somewhere in the neighbourhood of forty. He had a broad, flat head with sandy hair which had receded at the sides leaving a narrow peninsula of sparse growth down the middle. He wore horn-rimmed spectacles through which his eyes glinted sardonically, and his mouth was small, with lips which didn't seem to fit.

'Sorry to interrupt', he said amiably. 'But I've got to drive up to London this evening.'

'I was just leaving anyway', Manton replied, equally courteously, noticing the fluttering use the other made of a pair of well-manicured hands.

Spicer hesitated in the doorway and then said, with a certain air of diffidence, 'Would I be right in thinking you're one of the detectives from Scotland Yard?'

'You would, but how did you know?'

'Instinct', Spicer replied lightly, and added with a little laugh, 'Nothing to do with the size of your feet, I promise you.' There was the sound of a car being started up and he turned to go. 'That'll be mine. Be seeing you around the village, I expect. 'Bye.' And he gave Manton a casual flip of his hand as he walked off. A few seconds later, his M.G. swept out of the garage and disappeared down the lane.

Manton waited, but when Pringle failed to come back decided to go. He saw the garage man talking to his mechanic over by the bench, and realized then that he was intended to see himself off the premises.

As he pushed open the door of the police station on his return, he was greeted by a whining voice and sounds like a gramophone record being played backwards. Leaning against the counter he saw a small, extremely unhappy-looking man, who was the originator of the strange sounds. Beside him, surveying the scene with urbanity, was another man. This one had a rich black beard and, on his head, a royal blue turban.

Sergeant Yates, who was making efforts to pacify the smaller man, looked up as Manton entered.

'This man's called about Lucas, sir', he said. 'His name's Ajit Singh and he works on a farm near here. This other gentleman has come along as interpreter.'

The turbanned man nodded gravely. 'Ajit here,' he said, 'come to tell the police about the murder and claim the reward.'

The officers exchanged glances. Manton said, 'What does he know about the murder?'

'He see this . . . ' He turned to Ajit Singh and a fierce colloquy took place. 'This Lucas near the lady's house yesterday morning just before the murder was done. Now he would like to have the reward and go, please.'

Eventually with the aid of the interpreter, a more or less coherent statement was got out of Ajit, who sat throughout the proceedings alternately shivering and noisily clicking his finger joints. Working in the district he had heard about the murder and he had also heard Lucas's name being bandied round as the possible villain. His story was that he had come upon Lucas sitting against a hedge in one of his employer's fields around half-past eight the previous morning; and that Lucas had got up, climbed through the hedge and vanished when he, Ajit, approached.

While the statement was being written down, Manton had taken P.C. Green on one side and asked suspiciously:

'If the fellow doesn't speak any English, how much of this can we believe?'

'He can speak enough to get around, sir. I've heard him talk a bit of English when it suited him.'

'Where does he come from?'

'He works on a nearby farm, sir. He used to be employed in an engineering works, but I understand he developed some chest trouble and was told to get an open-air job.'

'I see. And what about the other fellow?'

'He's the self-appointed leader of the Indians in this area, sir. He's a clerk in one of those new factories out on the main road. He's better educated than the others: also speaks reasonably good English which most of them can't.' He paused thoughtfully. 'I'm pretty sure it's he who's suggested coming along, probably with the idea of going fifty-fifty. Ajit would never have had the brain to claim a reward.'

Manton grinned mischievously. 'Well, when we've got his statement signed, you're just the chap to tell them both that there isn't one anyway.'

FIVE

THE Steadmans had just finished supper, a somewhat frugal meal since Jane had become so absorbed with her story about Stanley and Moolie that she had forgotten to go to the shops until they were all closed. However, to make amends, she had dashed out to the off-licence and bought a bottle of Chablis and this they consumed with their scrambled eggs and cheese.

As Paul was carrying dirty plates out to the kitchen one by one and Jane was rushing from cupboard to cupboard looking for a tin of coffee which she was certain lurked hidden somewhere, the telephone rang.

'That'll probably be Linda Corby', she said. 'I told you she'd phone. Go and answer it, would you, darling.'

'If it's Linda, why don't you go', her husband replied, going off to fetch something further from the dining-room.

'Well, it probably won't be now.' Linda let out a small, exasperated sigh, had a final quick gaze round the kitchen for the missing tin of coffee and hurried off to the telephone, which seemed prepared to go on ringing till someone did answer it.

'Hello', she said in a dubious tone. 'Oh, it is you, Linda. I'd only just said to Paul that I must phone you this evening.'

'You've seen the papers, of course?' Linda Corby broke in breathlessly.

'Yes, I . . .'

'As you can imagine, it came as a tremendous shock to

both of us. I mean, murder, and after all, Richard was her nearest relative and we always felt a sort of responsibility for the old lady in a kind of way.'

'Yes, I'm . . .'

'Mind you, there's no point in pretending she was the easiest of persons to get on with. But at least Richard and I know in our consciences we couldn't have done more for her while she was alive.'

'No, I'm sure . . .' Jane tried again, but to no effect. Linda Corby had telephoned with the explicit intention of talking about her aunt's death, and talk about it she would, until she had said all she wanted. The somewhat unkind thought passed through Jane's mind that as soon as she was permitted to put down the receiver, Linda would lose no time in getting through to the next person on her list.

'Hello, hello, are you still there, Jane?' Linda's voice sounded fretful.

'Yes, yes', Jane said guiltily. 'I was . . .'

'That's all right. I thought we might have been cut off. As I was saying, she never really forgave me for not giving Richard any children; as if it was my fault! You know how much we spent on doctors' fees, and seeing that she never had any herself, well . . .' Jane clucked sympathetically and wondered how much longer she would go on. She tried to peep round the door to see whether Paul had taken over the search for the coffee. All she achieved, however, was to whip the cigarette box off the table with the telephone flex and scatter its contents over the floor.

'Richard's pretty certain the police know who did it', Linda was saying. 'It's only a matter of time before they catch him.'

'Oh, who do they think it is?' Jane asked eagerly.

'My dear, I don't think I ought to mention names over the telephone.'

'Oh!'

'Perhaps I *can* say it's someone who used to work for Aunt Sophie and whom she had to sack.'

'Oh.'

'A young man whom Richard never wanted her to employ because of you-can-guess-why.'

'Oh', Jane said again, this time uncomprehendingly.

'Richard doesn't think it'll be long before they arrest him and then you'll see his name in the paper. It begins with an "L". Quite a short name.' And then dropping her voice to a conspiratorial hiss she said, 'L-U-C-A-S. Look, dear, I mustn't talk to you any longer; there are a hundred and one things to be done, but I knew you'd want to let us have your sympathy at such a ghastly time. When the funeral and everything is all over, we must get together. Of course, we're going to be a little better off now', she threw in demurely as a postscript and with a brisk 'good-bye' rang off.

When Jane returned to the kitchen she found the dishes washed and the coffeepot bubbling.

'Oh, bless you, darling, you found it.' It didn't occur to her to ask where. 'It was Linda Corby. She says the police know who the murderer is and that his name is L-U-C-A-S.'

Her husband raised his eyebrows ever so slightly and said dryly, 'Let's hope then, that they f-i-n-d him.'

At about the very moment this observation passed Paul Steadman's lips, a small, worried looking man thrust his way into Five Meadows police station. P.C. Green was sitting in the office alone, diligently making out a firearms return. He looked up.

'Hello, Mr. Gawler. What's troubling you?'

'Jean's not come home', Gawler said in a flat, dazed tone.

Green looked up at the large clock which ticked noisily on the wall.

'It's only half-past eight. She may have gone to the pictures or something.'

The man shook his head. 'She said she'd be home her usual time. She leaves work at five and catches a bus which gets her back here a few minutes afore six. She weren't on it this evening.'

'Have you been in touch with the place where she works?'

'There wouldn't be no reply anyway. It's an office. It'd be shut.'

'Have you any reason to think she didn't go to work there as usual today?'

'No, she was there all right. I've just biked over to Bulstrode's farm. His daughter works in the same office. She says our Jean went to work today.'

'Do they usually come back together on the same bus?'

Gawler shook his head miserably.

'No, Mary Bulstrode cycles to work.'

Green scratched the back of his head. He knew what was in Gawler's mind; that his daughter had run off with young Lucas.

'Know if Jean's had a letter these last few days?' he asked.

'You spoke to her about it yourself last evening.'

'I know, and she told me she didn't know where he was.'

'It's my belief she did, Mr. Green.'

Green sucked in his lower lip. It was only a few hours ago that he had told Manton the contrary. Perhaps he had been too trusting after all; had accepted her word too easily. But she was a nice kid and he was always reluctant to accept that those whom he liked would deliberately deceive him. Perhaps that was why he wasn't yet a sergeant. He scratched the back of his head again.

'Well, all I can do, Mr. Gawler, is pass on what you've told me to the Yard officers and see what they think best. Meanwhile you'd better look in again before you go to bed and confirm she's still missing.'

'Aye, I'll do that, Mr. Green. Me and the missus are proper worried about her, I can tell you. Going off with the likes of him.'

'I don't expect she'll come to much harm wherever she is', Green said heartily.

'No, but mixing up with a . . . a murderer.'

'We don't know he's that yet.'

Gawler shot him an appraising glance.

'That's what everyone's saying. Mr. Pringle, he hasn't any doubts about it.'

'The law says no man is guilty until he's proved so by a jury', Green said stolidly. 'And we're still a long way off that happening. I don't like murderers any more than you do, but one doesn't want to brand young lads as such until a jury says they are. If Lucas killed Mrs. Easterberg, he'll deserve to get his neck stretched, but let's not have him convicted in advance by village gossip.' It was quite a speech and he had noticed Gawler's surprise increasing with each word he uttered. In an authoritative tone he now went on, 'All right, Mr. Gawler, you leave that with me. I'll let you know if we hear anything. Meanwhile tell Mrs. Gawler not to worry too much.'

When the news of Jean Gawler's disappearance was passed on to Manton, he looked thoughtful. After a while, he said, 'This may make it easier for us to find Lucas.'

Shortly afterwards orders went out to every police force in the country to be on the look-out for him.

The hunt for Dave Lucas was really on.

'You didn't ought to have come', the boy said, though without animosity.

'I wanted to help you, Dave.'

'You still didn't ought to have', he repeated like a catechism.

Dave Lucas was lying on his back on an old iron bedstead in the squalid little back room that had been his home for several days. His hands were clasped beneath his head which rested on an indescribably filthy pillow. He was wearing dark blue jeans and a light blue sweat-shirt. Sitting over in a corner of the room on the only chair was Jean Gawler. Her face was fresh and pretty and as yet untouched by the squalor of her surroundings. Her eyes seemed magnetically drawn and held by the still figure that lay on the bed, in particular by his round, almost cherubic face with the full lips and the long lashes which framed a pair of large brown eyes. He had once told her that his mother was Italian, since when Jean had pictured every male Italian having the same features as his.

He turned his head to glance at her and she gave him a wistful smile. But he immediately looked away again and resumed his contemplation of the yellow, fly-blown ceiling.

'I'll be able to go out and get things for you, Dave', she said eagerly, when the silence had become unbearable. 'It'll be much safer than your walking round the streets yourself. I'll be able to bring you the papers so you can see . . .' Her voice trailed away uncertainly.

'See what?' he asked from the bed without moving.

'See . . . well, see what's happening in the world.'

'See how close the police are on my tail, you mean.' But again he spoke without animosity.

'No, that wasn't what I meant, Dave', she said, with a slight catch in her voice. 'I know you didn't do it.'

This time he turned his head and held her gaze for several seconds. Then without speaking he fished a small comb out of his hip pocket and started to comb his long black hair. Jean watched him with absorption. She liked the big high crest in front he always gave to it. She liked too the smell of the dressing he put on it, even though it had once messed up her dress when he'd lain with his head in her lap. He wiped the comb on the pillow and put it away again.

'You're sure no one knows I'm here. You never told your mum or dad', he said abruptly.

'I promise I didn't, Dave. I never told a soul where you were, and I never left your letter about so they couldn't have seen from that. I've got it with me still.'

He nodded as though to accept her word. 'If there's any doubts about it, I've got to shift and shift fast.'

'There isn't, Dave.' She gazed at him with a bothered expression. 'Why have you got to hide like this, Dave, if you didn't do it?' she asked, in a tone devoid of guile.

'Why?' he said, viciously. 'I'll tell you why. Because I've got a record and because they'll say I had a motive to do the old girl in and because they've made up their minds I did it. That's why.'

She shivered at the cold ferocity of his tone and the sudden expression that had come into his eyes. She had never seen him look like this before and, for a fleeting moment, she felt scared at being alone with him in the empty house. She took a deep breath.

'But for how long?' she asked, in a frightened whisper. 'I mean, you can't spend the rest of your life hiding.'

With a sudden movement he swung his legs off the bed and sat facing her. Then he let out a long sigh.

'Look, Jean, I've already told you, you didn't ought to have come. But now you are here, will you please stop asking a lot of plaguing questions. I've got enough to worry about.'

She accepted the rebuke without any display of hurt feelings and went over to him. Resting a hand lightly on his shoulder she said, 'I'm sorry, Dave. I didn't mean to nag you.' He shook his head from side to side slowly as though unable to comprehend the female mind as she went on, 'I'm going to stay and look after you until it's all blown over and you don't have to worry any more.'

'Your mum and dad aren't half going to have something to say when you gets home.'

'I've posted them a letter saying not to worry.' Noticing the sudden look of alarm in his eyes, she added quickly, 'It's all right. I didn't post it anywhere near here.'

'What's the time?' he asked suddenly.

'Quarter past nine.' A reflective look came over her face. 'Funny to think I should be just arriving at the office. Wonder what they'll say when they hear I've disappeared.'

Lucas put out a hand and produced a cigarette packet from under the pillow. It was empty and he threw it across the room in disgust.

'I'll go out and buy some', the girl said eagerly.

'O.K.' He fished a ten-shilling note out of his pocket and flipped it at her. 'And for Christ's sake, be careful. And if you do think anyone's recognized you, make sure they don't trail you back here.'

'Don't worry, Dave. I'll be careful all right.' She bent her head down and he gave her a clumsy kiss. 'What are you going to do while I'm gone?'

'Think.'

He unlocked the door for her and re-locked it as soon as she was out in the narrow corridor. For a while he stood staring abstractedly at the farther wall. She was a nice kid all right and he was fond of her, but he still wished she hadn't come. This was the last time to be getting involved with a girl. He wondered how he could get rid of her, kindly but firmly; and above all safely. With a sigh he threw his chunky form back on the bed and stared once more at the ceiling.

Meanwhile Jean had crept down the rickety wooden staircase and let herself out of the back of the house. Coming cautiously round the side, she made sure that the street was deserted before emerging.

The house in which David Lucas had sought refuge was the end one in a terrace scheduled for demolition. Officially, that is so far as the local council was concerned, the lot of them were empty, but Jean had noticed, when she had arrived the previous evening, shadowy lights flickering in one or two of them. That, at any rate, was something which wouldn't give Dave away. He'd insisted that not even a match should be struck after it was dark.

The street, a short one, led into another almost as depressing and at the end of that lay a main road with shops and buses.

On the dozen or so occasions that Jean had been to London, it had been to Piccadilly Circus, Oxford Street and Buckingham Palace and around the West End and the shops in Kensington High Street. The London which she now saw was very different. It was grey and drab and friendless. If this was what was called North London, the people who lived there were more than welcome to it as far as she was concerned.

Trying to look inconspicuous she hurried along towards the shops. It had been a good idea tying a scarf over her head as it made her look almost like one of the locals, also made her face look different.

Tripping along with mounting confidence she rounded the corner into the main road and walked slap into the side of a policeman who was standing talking to a man who had a raincoat over his arm and a brown felt hat with the brim pulled well down.

Jean let out an involuntary gasp and stammered an apology. The policeman—he didn't look any older than Dave Lucas—grinned at her.

'That's all right, miss, as long as you're not hurt. Some of us are easier to bounce off than others.' He looked at the man with him and they exchanged a laugh.

Eyes cast down and feeling her cheeks burning, Jean hurried on. She crossed the street, not daring to look round, and hastened along the farther pavement. She passed at least two tobacconist's shops, but at the third went in and bought a packet of cigarettes. When she emerged she looked cautiously back towards the corner where the policeman had been. There was no sign of him and she gave a short sigh of relief. How silly she'd been to panic so easily. Policemen must be quite used to being bumped into, especially when they stood on busy street corners.

Mingling with the shopping crowds, she walked on, pausing occasionally to look into some window that took her fancy and to glance back and make sure that she wasn't being followed.

The food shops were the most crowded, full of women and prams and tugging children. Jean joined a queue in one of these and bought a couple of pies, some cheese and a loaf of bread. She was quite used to shopping for her family and had no difficulty in deciding what to buy. The pies were a lovely golden brown and everyone knew that cheese was full of vitamins.

Her shopping completed, she decided it was time to return to David. When he had had a meal, he would probably shake off his listlessness and tell her what they should do next.

On reaching the corner where the policeman had been and, before turning down the street that led to David's hide-out, she stopped to look in a shop window. She was rather pleased with this trick of pretending to admire a shop's wares, when in fact all you did was study the reflection in the glass. Not a policeman in sight. Not a single person paying her the slightest attention.

Five minutes later she was cautiously letting herself into the derelict house. The rotten boards creaked spookily beneath her feet. She arrived outside the back bedroom door, her heart beating faster, and knocked softly.

'It's me, Dave. I'm back.' She heard a faint sound within, then the door was unlocked and Dave's impassive face appeared in the crack as it opened. Quickly she slipped inside and he re-locked the door behind her.

'Here, look what I've bought, Dave', she said, displaying her purchases on the rancid bedcover.

Without looking at them, he asked nervously, 'Everything all right? You weren't spotted or anything?"

'Don't worry so, Dave. 'Course I wasn't spotted.' There was no point in telling him about her encounter with the policeman, as it would only set him worrying further and he was jumpy enough as it was.

Jean spread an old newspaper on the bed and set out their meal.

'Come on', she said in a coaxing tone. 'You must be hungry. I am.'

'Looks all right.' And he gave her a fleeting smile.

While they silently munched their way through the succulent meat pies, the man with the brown felt hat and the raincoat over his arm was standing across the street surveying the house with a thoughtful expression.

When the news reached Manton that a girl answering Jean Gawler's description had been seen and that it was thought she was with Lucas, he sent instructions that a watch was to be kept on the house but that the occupants were not to be disturbed until his arrival. Within a few minutes, he and Sergeant Yates were driving fast back into town.

Manton had done service with 'N' Division and knew the area well. As a young constable he had pounded the Stoke Newington beat for several years and there were few of its less salubrious streets which didn't evoke in him some memory or other, mostly of drunken brawls and of furious husband-wife quarrels on Saturday nights.

'Suppose he thought he'd be safer in these parts than south of the river where he belongs', he remarked, as their car cut deftly in and out of the traffic of London's northern suburbs.

'Given time, I bet we'll find he's been around the Elephant, though, sir; I imagine he left down there only after the murder. Didn't fancy going back, as he knew that was where we'd look first.' Manton nodded.

The car pulled up outside a drab stone building, over whose entrance hung the blue lantern which is every police station's identifying emblem.

Manton went inside only long enough to have a word with the head of the divisional C.I.D. and to pick up a local officer to guide him to the house where Lucas was believed to be.

'Think he may be armed?' the divisional Detective Superintendent asked.

Manton shook his head.

'No, I'm pretty sure not.'

'Too bad for someone if he is. I imagine you'll want some men to surround the place in case he makes a run for it.'

'Please. Assuming he hasn't got wind of us, I reckon half a dozen will be enough.'

'I had word from the officer watching the house about half an hour ago and he reported there hadn't been any further comings or goings.'

Ten minutes later, Manton, Yates and other officers were standing in the shadow of the house opposite Lucas's hideout. The officer who had been keeping observation said:

'I reckon he's in one of the rooms at the back, sir. The girl definitely went upstairs when she returned, and there hasn't been a sign of movement anywhere at the front since then, which was a couple of hours ago.'

'Did she go in through the front door?'

'No, sir. Somewhere round the back.'

'Then we'd better do the same', Manton said.

Satisfied that the house was surrounded and was under observation from every angle, he set off across the street, followed by Sergeant Yates and a local C.I.D. man. Moving quietly down the narrow passage which ran beside the half derelict house they reached a door which hung lopsidedly on one hinge.

Manton tested it gingerly and there was an angry scraping sound. Yates stepped forward and together they lifted it off the floor and swung it open sufficiently far to make their entrance into what had once been a kitchen but was now inches deep in dust and debris. Manton gazed up the decaying staircase and turned to Yates who was behind him.

'We'd better go up one at a time', he whispered. 'Make a note of the noisy stairs and avoid them when you come. If he comes out first, remember we rush him.'

But silence reigned upstairs and the minor sounds of their ascent evoked no reaction.

They paused, grouped together on the landing to take in their surroundings. Of the three doors which led from it, only one was firmly shut and, looking towards that, Manton was able to see that the dust in its vicinity had been disturbed by the traffic of feet.

With extreme caution he took a couple of paces to bring himself immediately outside the door. The other two did likewise and bunched themselves beside him.

He turned the handle quietly, but nothing happened. The three men exchanged a quick glance and then three shoulders went into action.

It was doubtful whether the door would in fact have stood up to one. As it was, they arrived inside the room with the eruptive force of a rugger scrum.

Like puppets jerked into movement, Lucas and Jean Gawler shot up from the bed on which they had been lying side by side asleep, their postures rigid in sudden panic. Then equally suddenly Lucas sighed, his shoulders slumped as though his bones had turned to melted wax.

'Oh, it's you', he said dully.

The girl, however, continued to stare, with a kind of stiff horror. It was almost a minute before there was any reaction, then she seemed suddenly to shrink as she buried her head in her lap and gave herself up to silent, agonizing grief. Lucas put out a hand to her, but without looking.

'Coming along to the station.' It was half question, half

injunction, and Manton's tone was quiet. Lucas swung his legs off the bed and stood up.

'What are we waiting for?' he asked, indifferently.

'Bring the girl too, Pete', Manton said to Yates. 'And get a message through to her parents as soon as possible.' He turned to the local C.I.D. officer. 'Have the car brought right up to the door, would you?' The officer nodded and left the room. A couple of minutes later he was back.

'Ready now, sir.'

Manton took a quick glance round the room. It looked completely devoid of personal belongings but he said, 'Got anything here you want to bring, Lucas?' Lucas shook his head wearily. 'Right, we'll be off then.'

The short drive to the police station was accomplished in total silence. Manton sat in the back between the two of them, but they neither looked at one another nor attempted to communicate. Just before they arrived, the girl became once more racked with heart-rending despair. Her body trembled violently and her breathing gave sounds of inconsolable anguish.

Leaving Sergeant Yates to put her in the care of a policewoman, he took Lucas along to the local Detective Superintendent's office. Its occupant was out but had left a message that Manton was to use the room.

'Hungry?' he asked, when they were both sitting. Lucas shook his head. 'Cigarette?' Lucas was about to take one, but drew his hand back.

'No', he said, sullenly.

Manton shrugged slightly and waited. A few minutes later, Sergeant Yates came into the room and sat down in the remaining chair and Manton said with quiet determination, 'And now, Dave, you and I are going to have a talk.'

SIX

But Lucas was no longer listening; indeed, he appeared unaware of his austere surroundings as he sat blinking with concentrated effort at the top of the desk. From time to time he compressed his lips and breathed out heavily through his nostrils.

'Better search him', Manton said, in an aside to Sergeant Yates. At the hideout they had done no more than satisfy themselves that he carried no arms. Now, before the interrogation began, was the time to find out whether some clue of more positive interest mightn't be secreted about his person.

'Stand up, Dave.' Sergeant Yates moved round behind Lucas's chair and playfully flicked the back of his neck. 'Empty your pockets.'

Lucas scowled and, after some initial fumbling, threw down on to the desk with affected indifference the contents of his pockets. He watched Manton take first the cheap, well-worn wallet and carefully go through its compartments. From out of these, he extracted a number of pound notes which he counted with the air of a fastidious bank clerk. In a quiet, neutral tone, he said, turning to Sergeant Yates, 'Twenty-two one pound notes, Pete. Better make a note of that.'

Lucas now watched him intently as he turned his attention to the other articles lying on the desk. A packet of cigarettes, a cheap lighter, a ball-point pen, some loose change; that was all, apart from a well-crumpled coloured handkerchief. Putting this on one side, he looked up and met Lucas's gaze.

'Those the clothes you were wearing the day before yesterday, Dave?' Lucas nodded. 'We shall have to find you some others then.' He paused and with a wry smile added, 'That is, I take it you have no objection to our having your clothes for laboratory examination?'

Lucas gulped. 'What for?' His voice came out as a croak, and both he and Manton knew that the question no more needed an answer than it had needed to be asked.

'Look, Dave, you know why we've brought you along here. Is there anything you'd like to tell us about the murder of Mrs. Easterberg two days ago?'

'I didn't have nothing to do with it.'

'You worked for her up until ten days ago, didn't you?'

'I'm not making no secret about it, am I?'

'And she sacked you?'

'I'm not the first person to be given the bloody sack, am I?'

'For dishonesty?'

'No! That's a bloody lie. I never had a thing off her.'

'Did you go back to the house the day before yesterday?'

'No, I didn't.'

'Where were you that day?'

'Here in London.'

'The whole day?'

'Yes, the whole day.'

'Ever been back to Five Meadows since you left Mrs. Easterberg's employ?'

'No.'

'Quite sure?'

'Positive.'

Manton nodded slowly, as though the answers accorded

with his own knowledge. Then, fixing Lucas with his bright blue eyes, he said in a conversational tone, 'Supposing someone says he saw you not far from Five Meadows Chase at about half-past eight in the morning the day of Mrs. Easterberg's murder, what would your answer to that be?'

This was a blow that landed and for a second Lucas looked scared. His hand moved towards the packet of cigarettes which lay on the desk and he was about to take one when Manton's own hand closed over them.

'What would be your answer to that?' he repeated.

'Who says he saw me there?' Lucas asked suspiciously.

'It doesn't matter *who* for the moment. But it's someone who's quite certain that it was *you* he saw.'

'Well, he's a something liar.' After a pause, he added, 'If he exists. I don't believe he does exist. If he did, you'd tell me his name. You're just trying to catch me out. You're like all the rest of 'em. You've got to pin this murder on someone and you've decided to pick on me. Now all you want to do is trap me, twist everything I say to make it sound worse in court.' His tone had been increasing in bitterness as he spoke and he now sat back, his cheeks glowing and his eyes burning with resentment.

'You haven't even been charged with anything yet', Manton remarked mildly. 'You're just deliberately working yourself up into a phony state of indignation. However I don't particularly mind whether you believe that someone saw you near the scene of murder or whether you don't. If you choose not to, that's your concern—though, in fact, I suspect you know it's true. The point is—and this is what *I* want to be quite certain about—you deny being there, or anywhere near Five Meadows, the day before yesterday: Is that right?'

'I've told you I wasn't there, I don't know nothing

about the murder.' The words were spoken, however, without conviction. Manton nodded and, removing his hand from the packet of cigarettes, tipped it in Lucas's direction. Lucas hungrily took one, accepted a light from Sergeant Yates and inhaled deeply.

Turning to Yates, Manton said, 'See if you can find us all a cup of tea, Pete. Also, get hold of some clothes for Dave. I'd like to get his to the lab as soon as possible.'

Sergeant Yates departed, to return to the room about five minutes later with an assortment of garments bundled under his arm.

'Here, try these, Dave', he said cheerfully, putting them down on a chair in the corner of the room.

'D'y'mean you want me to change now?'

'Yes, why not? Not bashful, are you? Mr. Manton and I'll look the other way if you're shy.'

Lucas scowled heavily and went across to where the clothes had been thrown down. Manton got up and in a tone which Lucas couldn't hear said to Yates:

'Handle the trousers carefully. Don't want to lose anything out of the turn-ups.'

Yates nodded and walked over to where Lucas was gazing at the clothes with a marked lack of enthusiasm.

'Come on, Dave. We've got you a real good outfit here.' One by one he handed the garments to the reluctant Lucas and accepted in return those which the youth now shed.

'You don't want me to take off my shoes as well, do you?' Lucas asked, when the change was otherwise complete.

'Shoes, too', Manton said, looking hard at the pair Lucas had on. Without bothering to bend down, Lucas levered them off and kicked them distastefully from him. With a patient sigh, Sergeant Yates picked them up and carefully dropped the pair he was holding on to Lucas's feet.

'Where'd that money come from, Dave?' Manton asked, when Lucas was finally reclothed. 'Twenty-two pounds. That's a lot of money, Dave.'

'I saved it.'

'Saved it?' Manton echoed with raised eyebrows.

'I won some of it at the dogs.'

'Now which? Saved or track winnings?'

Lucas hesitated a second. 'Both.'

'How much did you win?'

'I can't remember exactly.'

'About how much?'

'I can't remember.'

Manton's questions rained relentlessly about Lucas's ears. Which day? Which greyhound track? What was the name of the dog? What were the odds? And others, which sent him pitifully stumbling from one evasion to the next. At the end, Manton sighed and said simply, 'I think you stole the money from Mrs. Easterberg.'

'I never did.'

'We'll see.' It was said without malice or trace of vindictiveness. 'Don't mind staying here a bit longer, do you?'

'Not much choice, have I?'

Manton smiled and shrugged noncommittally. His mind went to the numerous occasions he had faced defending counsel from the witness-box and dealt deftly with a time-honoured line of questioning, which would run something like this:

'You say you hadn't cautioned the prisoner, officer?'

'That's correct, sir.'

'Why not? You'd made up your mind to charge him, hadn't you?'

'No, sir; not at that stage.'

'You'd made it clear from the questions you were asking him that you suspected him?'

'I can't say what impression he got from my questions, sir.' This said with a subtle mixture of blandness and deprecation.

'Come, officer, you're evading my question.'

At this point, there was quite often judicial intervention to halt what threatened to become a polemical interrogation. And finally, there came always this question.

'Are you really saying, officer, that if the prisoner had expressed the intention of walking out of the police station at that moment, he'd have been allowed to go?'

'It never arose, sir.'

'Never arose because you made it clear that he was in custody; that he couldn't go.'

'Oh, no, sir. He wasn't in custody. He hadn't been charged with anything.'

'Well, could he have walked out?'

'It's a hypothetical question, sir.'

'Even so, could he?'

'I'd have had no authority to prevent him, sir.'

At this point, counsel and witness both invariably cast their eyes towards the jury. From counsel, it was always a baleful look which said, 'See what a bunch of twisters the police are'. From Manton and his brother officers, an unwavering one of imperturbable fair-mindedness. That was the theme, but one, of course, susceptible of variations.

Leaving one of the station officers with Lucas, Manton and Yates made their way to a room upstairs where Jean Gawler was talking to a girl who looked very little older than herself and just as femininely attractive. She leapt up as the two men entered and introduced herself.

'Policewoman Ledgard, sir.'

Manton smiled at both girls.

'How are you feeling now, Jean?'

'All right', she said, in little above a whisper.

'We'll be sending you back home soon. We've notified your parents that you're safe and sound. I may even be able to drive you back myself. It all depends.'

'What about Dave?'

'What about him, Jean?'

'What are you doing to him? Are you letting him go too?'

'It's a bit early to say.' He was about to go on, when the girl broke in eagerly:

'Oh, please let him go. I know he had nothing to do with the murder. He's kind, he wouldn't kill anyone, he wouldn't hurt an old lady like Mrs. Easterberg. Please, please let him go home with me. He could get work at Five Meadows and I know Mummy would let him live at home with us.'

Manton looked down into her eager face with compassion. He wished she had never run away from home, even though she had been the instrument whereby Lucas had been found. She was an ordinary, simple country kid whom fate had decided to single out for a dose of hell. There was nothing new in a young girl becoming infatuated, but Manton recognized something sterling about her loyalty to the boy who was in trouble. This was more than the tempestuous tears of superficial emotion, and Manton earnestly wished he could wave a fairy-godmother's wand and put things right for her. Instead, he asked gently, 'Did he say anything to you about Mrs. Easterberg, Jean?' She shook her head. 'During the time you were with him in that room, didn't he mention the murder at all?'

'No. There was no need for him to, you see I told him I knew he had nothing to do with it.'

'And what did he say to that?'

'There wasn't anything for him to say, was there?'

Manton felt disarmed. Moreover, he believed what Jean had just told him. Whatever the rest of the world might feel about Dave Lucas, Jean Gawler had implicit faith in him. He turned to go.

'All right, Jean. Well, we'll soon have you home.'

With the questing, innocent gaze of a puppy, she watched him leave the room.

'Do you think they will let Dave go?' she asked hopefully as the door closed.

Policewoman Ledgard smiled reassuringly. 'Keep your fingers crossed for him, Jean, that's all you can do now.'

'I reckon we've got enough to charge him, don't you, sir?' Sergeant Yates remarked as he and Manton walked back to the room where they had left Lucas.

Manton expelled a noisy puff of breath and said dubiously, 'I suppose so, but I wish the identification was by someone other than that Indian. I don't like having a case which rests so much on someone whose English is negligible and whose motives seem to be primarily financial.'

'For all that, I think that Singh fellow was telling the truth. He knew Lucas quite well by sight and I don't believe he's just invented seeing him. And anyway, sir, there's quite a bit of additional evidence.'

'Such as?'

'All Lucas's obvious lies to us just now to account for his possession of the money. His motive; he'd been given the sack not long before and knew the old girl kept quite a bit of money about the house. He'd also have known that Wednesday was Miss Chatt's day off.'

'All those points you've just mentioned, Pete, are trimmings. The bits to garnish the main dish. But they're not of much weight on their own.'

'But they're not on their own, sir. There's the Indian's identification; also a strong possibility of our getting some evidence out of the laboratory.'

'More or less what was passing through my mind. Let's go down to the Yard now and see if we can squeeze some information out of someone at the lab.'

Before departing, Manton stuck his head round the door of the room where Lucas was sitting dejectedly and gave instructions to the officer with him. Looking over towards Lucas, he added, 'Can you fix him a meal?'

Twenty-five minutes later their car turned off Whitehall and came to rest outside the headquarters of the Metropolitan Police, New Scotland Yard. In a few minutes they were talking to Inspector Povey, who was one of the laboratory's liaison officers.

'Here's some more stuff in the Five Meadows case, Arthur', Manton said, handing over the series of polythene bags into which Lucas's belongings had been packed. 'Any chance of having a word with the Director now?'

'He's up to his neck in work', Inspector Povey replied guardedly.

'I'm sure he is; but this is urgent, Arthur.'

'You're not expecting him to examine this stuff while you wait, are you?' The inspector's tone was shocked.

'Not all of it', Manton said blandly, and went on, 'Has he started to look at the stuff the county police brought in yesterday?'

'You mean the various specimens and samples from the scene and from the dead woman?' Manton nodded. 'I think he may have. As you know, he usually gives priority to murder jobs.'

'Well, perhaps I could have a short word with him?'

There was a silence during which the two officers stood in mutual appraisal.

'What exactly is it you want to know? It'd be much better if you didn't bother him now. He'll let you have his report as soon as he possibly can, and you'll only be delaying yourself if you stop him working.'

Manton took a deep breath. 'Look, Arthur, you're a wonderful watchdog and I'm sure the lab boys get a lot more work done thanks to your protecting them against interruptions, but this is something really urgent. On it may depend whether or not we charge someone with this murder. Moreover, I think it's probably something the Director could answer very quickly.' He paused and turned to the table on which Lucas's clothing had been placed. Picking up the two bags which contained his shoes, he went on, 'All I want to know is whether either of these shoes fits the plaster cast you have of the footprint that was found in a flower bed.'

Inspector Povey pursed his lips, then turning on his heel, he said, 'I'll go and have a word with the Director.' When he reappeared, it was to beckon them after him.

Dr. Renshaw, the Director of the Metropolitan Police laboratory, was a tall, lean man with a pronounced stoop who was wont to give evidence standing on one leg, the other being somehow wound round the first in what appeared to be a posture of exquisite discomfort. So poised, he stood over a workbench when Manton and Yates were shown in.

'Trying to rush me as usual?' he said, turning his head in their direction rather like a flamingo.

'I expect Inspector Povey explained the urgency, Dr. Renshaw.'

'Still no reason to try and make me skimp my work and give you snap judgments. If some poor fellow's fate is in the balance, all the more reason to proceed with caution. Don't you agree?'

'Entirely.'

'Liar', Dr. Renshaw replied pleasantly and, uncoiling his leg, loped away to the far end of the bench.

The three officers followed and watched him carefully remove each shoe from its transparent container. He studied them with the attention of a craftsman cobbler for several seconds and, then holding a shoe in one hand and the plaster cast in the other, he patiently juggled them together, later repeating the process with the other shoe.

'Wasting my time like this!' he muttered as he laid them back on the bench. Suddenly swivelling his head round, he barked out, 'Don't need a scientist to tell you that this footprint'—he stabbed a bony finger towards the cast—'was made by this left shoe. Any idiot can see it was. Even a jury could!'

When they got back to the police station in north London, they found Lucas fed and sitting back in his chair idly watching the smoke curl upward from the cigarette which dangled between his lips. His body stiffened as Manton and Yates entered the room and his eyes went anxiously from one face to the other.

'Come on, Dave, we're taking you to Five Meadows', Manton said in a brusque tone.

Lucas rose slowly to his feet and stood in an attitude of quiet submission, and Manton went on formally. 'I must tell you that you'll be charged there with the murder of Mrs. Sophie Easterberg.' He paused. 'So you're now under caution, Dave. You know what that means, don't you? I don't have to explain the caution to *you*, do I?'

'Answer the Superintendent when he speaks to you, Dave', Sergeant Yates said, taking a step forward. 'He's asking you what you'd like to say. This is the time when those who've got any brains in their heads decide to tell the truth. We'd most likely be able to help you if you did that.'

Lucas shook his head like a child determined to fight back tears.

'I didn't murder her', he muttered in a tight voice.

'The truth, Dave, I said. Lies'll only get you into worse trouble.'

There was a silence and then Manton said with finality. 'All right, we don't want to waste time.' He turned to Yates. 'Better arrange for the girl to be sent home in another car. We can't give her a ride now. Also phone up Superintendent Blaker and tell him we're bringing Lucas back'—he looked at his watch—'and should be at Five Meadows just inside the hour. Explain to him what's happened.'

Sergeant Yates left the room, to return about ten minutes later. While he was away Manton propped himself against the wall beside the door and observed Lucas with calm, watchful eyes. Neither of them uttered a single word. Indeed, Lucas seemed so preoccupied with his own thoughts as to be oblivious of his surroundings. Not for the first time Manton had occasion to wonder at his apparent powers of concentration, and would have given much to be able to penetrate his thoughts. His eyes were fixed on some invisible horizon and a frown flickered on and off his face like summer lightning, as he stood motionless, fingertips of one hand resting lightly on the edge of the desk.

'Everything's fixed, sir', Yates announced on his return. He looked at Lucas and then back at Manton with raised eyebrows. Manton shook his head. He knew that his sergeant expected him to have put the time to practical use, but it was he, not Yates, who would have to stand up to cross-examination in the witness-box. Moreover, though he was dealing with a Borstal boy with a criminal record, Manton felt disinclined to employ any of the tricks which are sometimes regarded as fair on such occasions.

When they arrived at Five Meadows, they found a line of cars parked outside the police station. Taking Lucas firmly by the arm, Sergeant Yates hurried him up the short path while Manton followed behind ready to protect their charge from any press photographers who might suddenly appear in their path.

Inside the station, Superintendent Blaker, Sergeant Spruille and P.C. Green were sitting about in attitudes of bored inactivity. Manton quickly explained the position again and while Blaker went across to the phone to make the necessary arrangements with the clerk to the justices, he, Yates, and P.C. Green huddled together with Lucas in another corner of the tiny office. Green had been deputed to prefer the charge and this he now proceeded to do with theatrical solemnity.

'David Lucas, I charge you for that you on the twenty-second day of May at Five Meadows did murder Sophie Easterberg against the Peace of our Sovereign Lady the Queen, her crown and dignity. I must warn you that you are not obliged to say anything in answer to the charge but that whatsoever you do say will be taken down in writing and may be given in evidence.'

He paused, red-faced and out of breath, and Sergeant Yates gave Manton a wink. But Lucas himself made no response; his face was pale and expressionless.

Five Meadows Magistrates' Court was almost an anachronism. It normally sat but once a month and on those occasions its business was completed before lunch.

The courthouse itself was an annexe to the grey stone police station and consisted of a small room with a raftered ceiling and a number of narrow tables and cast-out chairs. It never lost its cold, dusty, disused smell, and like so many courthouses had been designed by someone who had small conception of the requirements.

About half-past five that afternoon, Mr. Smalley, a local farmer and a justice of the peace, took his seat on the bench and nodded amiably at everyone present. Mr. Talbot, who was the clerk of the court, adjusted his spectacles for the hundredth time and nervously cleared his throat. No one had appeared in his court charged with murder since the year after Queen Victoria died and he felt the present occasion weighing upon him.

'David Lucas', he said in a worried tone, looking anxiously at every face save that of the youth who stood in the ridiculous play-pen which passed as a dock. There was an awkward pause as though no one knew their lines and then Superintendent Blaker stood up.

'Your Worship,' he said, 'I ask for a remand in this case. The police have further inquiries to make and the matter is one which has to be referred to the Director of Public Prosecutions.'

He sat down again and all eyes turned on Mr. Talbot, who was dreamily sucking the end of his pen.

'What comes next?' Mr. Smalley asked, peering over the top of his desk at the clerk's head of bushy white hair.

Mr. Talbot brought his worried gaze to bear on Dave Lucas. 'Well, er . . . Lucas, well you've heard what the er . . . the Superintendent has said. He's er . . . asking for a remand. Have you any objection to that?' When Lucas shook his head, Mr. Talbot let out an audible sigh of relief. 'Well . . . er . . . then, sir,' he went on, cricking his head round to address Mr. Smalley, 'would you remand him in custody for . . . er . . . eight days.'

'That'll be a Sunday', hissed Blaker.

'No, no, a Saturday, surely . . .'

Diaries were brought out and consulted, and after a further colloquy during which Lucas exhibited signs of extreme boredom, the remand date was fixed. In the silence which followed, he said, 'I'd like legal aid.'

Mr. Smalley nodded his assent. 'You'll arrange that will you, Mr. Talbot?'

'Yes, sir. I thought of assigning him Mr. Macready', Mr. Talbot replied, shooting a mildly triumphant glance at Superintendent Blaker.

Blaker tossed his head petulantly. 'He would', he snorted in Manton's ear. 'I suggested some nice old fogies to him over the phone, who'd have been much better.'

'From whose point of view?'

'Whose do you think?'

'What's wrong with Macready?'

'Too eager and enthusiastic by half', Blaker said disgustedly. 'He'll try and make trouble from the word go. Likes attacking the police too.' His tone became indignant. Manton decided, however, to reserve his own judgment on Lucas's solicitor until they met. He knew that the popular police idea of a good defending lawyer was one who asked no questions in the preliminary stages of a hearing and who acquiesced in everything the police suggested. Such compliance could, in his view, be overdone, as for that matter could its converse. Manton hoped that Mr. Macready's scorned enthusiasm didn't necessarily put him in the latter class.

A few minutes later Mr. Smalley had retired to the small box of a room behind the bench which served as the justices' retiring room. Mr. Talbot followed him with the warrant which, when signed, would authorize the governor of Her Majesty's prison at Brixton to take care of Lucas for the next eight days.

'You don't like Blaker, do you?' Mr. Smalley said casually as he put his signature to the document.

'He's as tactful as a steamroller', Mr. Talbot replied, tartly.

'I'm glad Macready's going to defend. I take it you've already spoken to him about the case.'

Mr. Talbot nodded. 'I did so immediately after Blaker had told me over the phone whom he thought I should give the defence to.'

'Whom did he suggest?' Mr. Smalley asked, with twinkling amusement.

'Frodsham amongst others.'

'Good God! He's never had a client whom he hasn't advised to plead guilty.'

'I know. He's also very deaf now.'

The two men looked at each other and laughed.

Manton went along to the police station cell where Lucas was lodged before being driven to the prison.

'Anyone you want me to see for you?' he asked.

'What d'you mean?' Lucas's tone was puzzled.

'Any family you want notified about things? Parents, for instance.'

'Haven't got none.'

'Family then?'

'No thanks. I've only got an aunt and she won't want to have anything to do with me now. She never did much, anyway.'

Manton pulled out his cigarettes and tossed one to Lucas, who caught it neatly.

'You still hoping to get me to confess?' he asked suspiciously. 'Because it won't work; I'm going to fight you the whole bloody way. You'll have to prove the lot, *and* without any help from me. And you can give that in evidence if you want.'

'O.K. Dave, don't yell at me', Manton said mildly.

'No, but I know you lot. You and your twisting ways.'

'Look just because you've been to Borstal, you don't know all the answers, so pipe down. If I'd wanted to get a confession out of you, I'd have done it almost without your noticing.'

Lucas made a scoffing sound, and Manton turned to go.

'Who's this Macready bloke?' Lucas suddenly asked. 'Is he any good?'

'The best.'

'Why did that other super of yours tell me to ask for an old basket called Frodsham then?'

Manton shrugged his shoulders but found it not hard to guess at the answer.

That night, as Dave Lucas lay in an austere hospital bed at Brixton prison in south-east London, not three-quarters of a mile from where he had been born, the case entered on a new phase.

SEVEN

PAUL STEADMAN fingered the bulging pink folder, bound with a piece of white tape, which lay in front of him on his desk. On the outside of the folder in large printed capitals was written, 'The Queen against David Lucas'. Below came the information that the file had been submitted by the Commissioner of Police of the Metropolis: that it concerned the offence of murder: that the venue of the offence was Five Meadows Magistrates' Court: and that Detective Superintendent Manton of New Scotland Yard, extension number 086, was the officer in charge of the case.

Steadman gave a gentle pull at the neat bow with which the white tape was tied and opened the folder. Like a dog that first picks out the tit-bits from its plate, he extracted the album of photographs from the bottom of the pile and began thumbing through them. The first was a fine house agent's view of Five Meadows Chase showing the aspect which took in Mrs. Easterberg's bedroom windows. Next there was a close-up of the flower-bed and trampled tulips beneath her bedroom windows, which was followed by one of the sill on which scratch marks could be clearly seen. For the fourth, the photographer had moved into the bedroom and stayed there to take a further seven photographs, several of which showed Mrs. Easterberg lying on the floor in the position in which she had been found by the police. The last three in the album were of the landing, staircase and front hall.

Steadman turned his attention to a second, smaller album which contained close-ups of Mrs. Easterberg's injuries taken during the course of the post-mortem examination. They were neither more nor less pleasant than their kind. For some years it had been the practice to bind the mortuary photographs separately, since judges had a habit of inquiring, in the tone of voice of an outraged parent, whether it was really necessary for the jury to see them. Steadman gazed at them without emotion, though he always hoped that his own body would be spared the indignity of being butchered after death.

After the photographs, he studied a scale plan of the two floors of Mrs. Easterberg's house which a police draughtsman had carefully prepared. He preferred when he could, however, to avoid using plans in court, as their size invariably provoked judicial criticism. They were either too large and enveloped the judge or else they were too small and he couldn't see what was on them. If they did happen to be an approved size, then almost certainly they failed to show the very thing the judge thought most important.

Refolding the plan, Steadman paused to make menacing noises at a pigeon that was strutting up and down his window ledge. It flew off after registering a look of mild surprise at the lack of welcome.

Steadman turned back to the file and started reading. He had almost finished when Tom Coles stuck his head round the door.

' 'Lo, Paul. Hear you've got the Five Meadows case. That it you're reading?'

'Yes.'

Coles picked up the photographs and flipped through them. They might have been the pages of a seed catalogue which held small interest for him.

'Straightforward case?' he asked, dropping the album of photographs back on Steadman's desk.

'Mmm, I think so.'

'Chap made a confession?'

'No.'

'Must mean the police are satisfied with the evidence they've got then.'

Paul Steadman smiled. Such cynicism was common amongst the members of the department. One had to grow a protective skin of some sort when the criminal law was one's living; otherwise the seaminess would sooner or later get one down.

'We've got his footprint in a flower-bed below the deceased's windows and a witness who saw him in the area about the time of the crime.'

'Reliable?'

'Who, the witness?' Coles nodded. 'An Indian.'

'Ha!' Tom Coles said with zest. 'Foreign witnesses always make a case more of a lottery than it normally is. Especially Indians. They regard truth like a football, to be given a good hearty booting around. They don't really mean to lie, it's just that they view the matter somewhat differently; and of course they're morbidly fascinated by the process of law.'

'Lucky I've got the footprint then.'

'What other evidence is there?'

'There's a postman named Sam Shoe, who proves the time of the offence—by inference, that is. He went to the house shortly before ten o'clock and couldn't get any reply, which means the old lady must have been dead by then.'

'She might have been in the lavatory.'

'Sam Shoe thought of that too, and gave her time to appear.'

Coles nodded approvingly. 'Must have known he might be required to give evidence. I don't know about you, Paul, but I always find it's the short witnessses like Sam Shoe whose evidence so often becomes whittled away until you wonder why on earth you ever called them.'

'I know, and with a skilfully conducted defence it's only afterwards you realize how erosive the effect has been.'

'Incidentally, I've never asked you, but was the deceased the aunt of Jane's schoolfriend?'

'Yes. She's not a witness, though.'

'What about her husband?'

'He is, but I've never met him. Nor has Jane for that matter, so I don't foresee any embarrassment. Moreover, his evidence isn't likely to be controversial.'

'Do you know who's defending?'

'A solicitor named Macready. Heard of him?'

'No.'

'Superintendent Manton says the local police don't care for him.'

'That means Blaker, I suppose! He doesn't like anyone who doesn't fall in with everything he wants.' Coles stretched and smothered a yawn. 'Well, I wish you joy with the case, Paul.'

Steadman gazed pensively at the far wall. 'On the face of it, it's straightforward enough,' he said, 'though there are one or two odd features about the evidence. Know what I mean, Tom? One has no doubt it's a true bill, but one or two bits just don't seem to fit together properly.'

At the same time that Steadman and Coles were conducting a somewhat desultory conversation about the case, James Macready was sitting facing Dave Lucas in one of the interview rooms at Brixton prison. In sight but out of earshot sat a prison officer.

'Thought I'd drop in and see you, even though there's not much we can do for the time being.' Lucas nodded meekly and Macready went on, 'Between now and the hearing next week, I'd like you to write me out your life history.' He looked up with an infectious grin. 'Tell me as much about yourself as you can. You've got nothing else to do all day, so it'll help pass the time.'

'O.K., sir', Lucas murmured, though without enthusiasm.

'Fine. I'll be off now. If there's anything you want, drop me a line. In any event I'll probably get my clerk to pay you a visit in a day or so to take a preliminary proof of your evidence. He's already been nosing around Five Meadows to see whether there's anything useful to your defence to be found there.'

'What about Jean, sir?'

Macready frowned. 'I think the prosecution are certain to call her as a witness.' Observing Lucas's alarmed expression, he went on, 'Doesn't mean she's turned against you, but they'll want her evidence to prove where you were and what you were doing during the time she was with you. But don't worry, she'll still be able to assist us under cross-examination. We know what she's told the police, because she came along to my office and repeated word for word the statement she'd given them. No, you needn't worry about her.'

James Macready, who was short and slight with dark, curly hair, had a normally serious expression which now relaxed into a smile as he took off his spectacles. At thirty-two he was the junior partner in a prosperous firm of solicitors; a position he had reached by dint of sheer hard work. He had a considerable flair for criminal defence work and he exerted all his not inconsiderable energy in every case which he undertook.

'Anything else you want to ask before I go, Lucas?'

'How much should I tell the prison doctor, sir? He's already interviewed me a couple of times.'

'About the crime, you can tell him as much as you've told me. Namely that you don't know anything about it because you didn't do it. That's what you've said all along, isn't it?'

' 'S'right, sir, because that's the truth.'

Macready nodded briskly. 'He's been interviewing you because in due course he has to make a report on whether you're sane and fit to stand your trial, etcetera.'

'They're not going to try and put me in Broadmoor?'

'Good heavens, no. Yours isn't going to be a medical defence. It's going to be a straight fight on the facts.'

'What do you think my chances are, sir?'

Macready paused in mid-motion of putting his papers back into his briefcase.

'I'm not going to answer that except to say they're a darned sight better than those of most men charged with murder, simply because you've not made a statement to the police.'

Lucas put up a hand and nervously fingered his lower lip.

'If I should be convicted, it's a hanging job, isn't it?'

'If they prove it was murder done in the course of theft, yes, it is. But don't think along those lines.' He met Lucas's gaze. 'Have you ever done any boxing?'

'Yes; quite a bit at one time', Lucas said, puzzled.

'You had to train before a fight, didn't you?' Lucas nodded slowly and the solicitor went on, 'Well, that's what you've got to do now. Toughen yourself up in readiness for the case. When you go into court, it'll be like going into the boxing ring. I'm your manager. It's my job to ensure you're as fit as you can be by the time you come up for trial. The hearing in the magistrates' court is only a preliminary bout in which we sit and watch the other side do a bit of shadow work. Now the first thing a fighter needs is confidence. Confidence in himself and in those who are trying to help him. O.K?'

The tension seemed to go out of Lucas. Macready had achieved his purpose. As he turned to go, Lucas said, 'I didn't kill the old lady, sir, and that's the honest truth.'

Macready paused and looked back over his shoulder. 'It's the jury who've got to be convinced of that.'

EIGHT

HIS lay friends frequently asked Paul Steadman what the various people he had prosecuted looked like, their interest usually being confined to those who had been charged with murder. He was generally able to satisfy their curiosity, though not as easily as might be expected, for he had occasionally spent hours in court without ever catching a glimpse of the person he was prosecuting, thanks to the peculiar construction of the courthouse.

More often than not, the prisoner sits behind the opposing advocates, who have their back to him, and when in addition he is immured in a dock, apparently designed to thwart an escaping kangaroo, very little of him shows over the top anyway.

All this, therefore, makes difficult any study of the accused round whom the forensic battle is being waged.

Five Meadows Magistrates' Court, however, did not present this problem, since the dock was a small area in the middle of the floor marked off by low railings of purely token value.

The designer of Five Meadows court had shown rarer and more astonishing initiative by positioning the witness-box behind the level of the seats occupied by the lawyers. This meant that a hapless advocate either faced the justices and hoped his questions would bounce back off the wall behind them and be picked up by the witness; turned his back on the justices, with the result that he almost rubbed noses with the witness and felt constrained to conduct a whispered interrogation which no one else in the court room had a chance of hearing; or, facing his front, threw his questions over one shoulder like a horse trying to reach the bottom of its nosebag.

When the time came Paul Steadman had decided on this last technique, but was more than relieved when Mr. Talbot directed an improvised witness-box to a position more convenient for all concerned.

He arrived at court, as was his custom, a good twenty minutes before the case was due to be heard. This gave him time to sort out his papers and spread them around like someone about to play patience. Space was his essential and without it he always felt miserably fettered in his task of exposition.

On the day of the Lucas case, Manton met him by car at the main line station six miles away and drove him over to court.

'That's The Chase where Mrs. Easterberg lived, sir', Manton said, pointing, when their car approached the village.

A couple of minutes later, they pulled up outside the police station. As they did so, another car did likewise and Dave Lucas got out, escorted by two men in prison officers' uniform. He paused on the pavement looking about him while one of the officers spoke to the driver. He appeared at ease and said something to his other escort, who smiled and shrugged his shoulders.

'He doesn't look like a young thug', Steadman said, turning to Manton in the car.

'They don't always.'

'But he's got rather a pleasant, open face.'

'He's not a bad boy, sir; if you can forget he's committed a particularly brutal murder.'

Steadman shot Manton a sidelong glance, but it didn't seem that the superintendent was being deliberately sarcastic. Indeed he was probably being quite sincere, Steadman thought. Police officers often did come to like the men whom they had arrested. Strange bonds of matiness would develop, a sort of inverted comradeship in arms whereby the officer would do what he could to ease the other's journey on the way to prison or gallows, though all the while determined to get him there.

'Want to have a word with any of the witnesses, sir?' Manton asked, opening the car door his side and stepping out.

'No thanks. And particularly not Captain Corby. He's the one I told you about whose wife knows mine. I'll speak to him afterwards, but I don't want to see him before he's given his evidence.'

Manton smiled. It always amused him the way the D.P.P.'s representatives shied away from any suggestion that they might care to interview any of the lay witnesses before a case. They reacted like maiden ladies to obscene invitations.

The courtroom was already fairly full when they pushed their way through to the front. A number of national newspapers had sent down men to cover the case, despite its lack of sex interest. Brutality by young men against old ladies was still reasonably good copy and a useful editorial peg on which to hang any number of different viewpoints.

Mr. Talbot, who was fussing with sheets of paper, looked up as Steadman put down his briefcase on the far side of the big table across which clerk and advocates faced each other.

They stretched over and shook hands.

'Think you'll finish in the day?' Mr. Talbot asked.

Steadman appeared to consider for a second. 'I should

think so. Depends a bit on how much the defence cross-examine.' It was one of three replies he was wont to give to this particular question. This was the cautious variation used on occasions when he thought he might be going to have a rough passage.

'I have three justices sitting', Mr. Talbot went on. 'Mr. Smalley, Mrs. Grace and Mr. Bitterson.'

Steadman nodded with polite interest.

'Mr. Bitterson's new', Mr. Talbot added.

'Oh.' But this came out with the wrong inflection and Steadman hastily added, 'Sounds like a well-balanced bench.'

'Two farmers and a farmer's wife!' Mr. Talbot looked at his watch. 'I wonder if Mr. Macready's ready. If so, we'll get started.' He looked about the courtroom. 'Find out if Mr. Macready's ready, will you, Superintendent', he called across to Blaker.

When Macready had taken his seat, he leaned across to Steadman and said, 'Glad to meet you on rather more even ground than the defence usually meet the prosecution in a murder case.'

'Are you going to cross-examine much at this stage?'

'I'm not sure yet. I shall wait and hear what you say in your opening.'

The two advocates exchanged steely smiles as a voice called out, 'Rise, please.'

Mr. Smalley, Mrs. Grace and the new Mr. Bitterson came through a door at the rear of the bench and took their seats. Mr. Talbot, who had gone to fetch them, hurried round to his place and sat down.

The door which led direct into the police station opened and Dave Lucas came through and stepped into the ridiculous dock. He looked young, plump-faced and innocent. Those who could stared at him with consuming interest: none more so than Lewis Spicer, who had got himself into a vantage point from which the occupant of the dock was under his perpetual scrutiny.

Mr. Talbot cleared his throat and nervously opened the proceedings.

'You know the nature of the charge against you, Lucas. And today you have the advantage of being represented by Mr. Macready, who will be able to question the witnesses on your behalf. I'm sure he's explained to you what today's proceedings are, but I think I should just quickly tell you again.' Mr. Talbot removed his spectacles and then put them back on again. 'You're not being tried here today. This is just the preliminary hearing of your case. The prosecution will call their witnesses and at the end, the justices will decided whether or not there is evidence to justify your being committed for trial before a judge and jury at a higher court. Do you understand all that?'

Lucas, who had been watching Mr. Talbot with pursed lips, nodded gravely.

'Very well then, you may be seated.' Mr. Talbot himself sat down, glanced back towards the justices as though to make sure they had not suddenly evaporated, and gave Paul Steadman his cue.

Steadman rose, waited, like a great conductor, for complete silence and began his opening speech.

'May it please your worships, I appear in this case on behalf of the Director of Public Prosecutions and the accused, David Lucas, is defended by my friend Mr. Macready.' He took a breath and was about to continue when Mr. Talbot suddenly interjected, 'Are all witnesses out of court? Very well, yes, go on please, Mr. Steadman.'

Paul Steadman permitted himself a faint frown of disapproval. He disliked such interruptions, regarding them as undignified and unflattering. His attitude was that of an actor's towards rattling teacups at a matinee. Fixing Mr. Talbot with a coldly subduing look, he took a fresh breath and continued, 'The accused, who is twenty years old, comes before the court charged with the murder of Sophie Easterberg. Mrs. Easterberg, who was seventy-four years old, lived at Five Meadows Chase on the outskirts of this village. She was found dead in the bedroom of her house at about five o'clock on the evening of Wednesday, the twenty-second of May. In the opinion of Doctor Innes, who performed a post-mortem examination, she had been dead for several hours before the discovery of her body. Indeed, from the evidence which you will hear, it is apparent that she had been killed somewhere between half-past nine and ten that morning and had then lain in the empty house until her nephew, Captain Corby, arrived there seven hours later.' He paused and turned a page of his notebook. 'There will be evidence before you that the accused used to work for Mrs. Easterberg; and what the crown allege is that he murdered her, murdered her moreover in the course or furtherance of theft: that he went to her house to steal and killed her when she surprised him in the act of theft.'

For the next fifteen minutes or so, Steadman expanded his observations and outlined the evidence which the witnesses would be called to give. He did so factually and without rhetoric; a speech more in the style of a Chancellor of the Exchequer presenting his budget than of a vote-swinging candidate at an election. The court listened attentively, except for Lucas himself, who soon became bored and started cleaning his nails with the pencil which Mr. Macready had given him for taking notes.

Paul Steadman now turned the last pages of his own notes. 'Before calling my witnesses,' he went on, 'I ought to say something about the medical evidence. As you will shortly hear, the actual cause of death in this case was suffocation; not the blow on the head which Mrs. Easterberg received. Dr. Innes will tell you that the blow from the poker must have rendered her unconscious, but that she died from falling or lying face downwards in the soft cushion which was found beneath her head.' Steadman shifted his weight and, leaning forward, said with compelling earnestness, 'Whether the cushion was already on the floor, as a result of the skirmish which obviously took place before the accused overcame Mrs. Easterberg, or whether the accused, for some reason known unto himself, subsequently placed it under her head after she had fallen, makes, in the crown's submission, no difference in law to this charge.' He was aware of Mr. Macready on his right casting him a sharp glance as he proceeded to enlarge upon this legal aspect of the case. He concluded, 'So that either way, what the accused did amounts in law to murder.' He was now nearing the end of his opening remarks.

'In brief therefore, your worships, the crown say that there is ample evidence—strong circumstantial evidence—to prove that it was this man, Lucas, who murdered Mrs. Easterberg, and that he did so in the course or furtherance of theft. If that is your view when you have heard all the evidence, then it will be your duty to commit him to take his trial upon this charge.' He slowly removed his spectacles, relaxed his posture and said, 'And with those observations, I will now call the evidence before you.'

There was a general rustle in court as he finished speaking.

Dave Lucas looked up with momentary interest and then resumed his toilet. The justices started whispering together and Mr. Talbot rearranged his papers for the umpteenth time. Macready leaned across to Steadman and said in a confident whisper, 'That's quite a subtle point of law you've raised.'

'Nothing in it for you, though', Paul Steadman replied blithely.

'Don't be so sure! I can see your case on quicksands already.'

Steadman grinned. 'If it comforts you to think so, go ahead. But it's my bet that in the end you'll be glad to try and get a verdict of insanity.'

'You hope! I've never heard so much theorizing as there was in your opening. You've scarcely a couple of facts to rub together!'

It was with the glint of battle in their eyes that the two advocates turned back to their respective papers. The justices now ceased whispering and Mr. Talbot looked in Steadman's direction.

The first witness, a police photographer, was called and entered the box. He handed round albums of the photographs which he had taken, to the justices, Mr. Talbot and Mr. Macready. Steadman had already been supplied with them. The nearer spectators now craned their necks in vain attempts to see the albums' contents. The first album comprised photographs of the scene of the crime; the second showed close-ups of Mrs. Easterberg's injuries, which the justices studied with calm interest.

Mr. Macready had no questions to ask the photographer, and this witness was quickly succeeded by the plan-drawer, who produced the fruits of his labours, which was a large, unwieldy plan of the interior of Five Meadows Chase. The court accepted with some relief Paul Steadman's suggestion that there was no need to refer further to it at the present stage and set about folding their copies, rather in the manner of disengaging from a bear's hug.

'I will now call Miss Violet Chatt', Steadman announced, with the air of a compère who has warmed his audience up.

Miss Chatt was ushered, took the oath in a nervous tone, put her right glove back on and gazed expectantly at Mr. Talbot.

'Is your full name Violet Chatt?' Paul Steadman asked her. She started guiltily and swung her head to see where the question came from. There followed several more as formal, before Steadman said, 'You were, I think, Mrs. Easterberg's companion at the time of her death?'

'That's right. I'd been with her about nine months.'

'Would you just look a moment at the man in the dock.' Miss Chatt did so. 'Do you recognize him?'

'Yes. It's David Lucas.'

'Do you know him?'

'Only from his having been employed for a time by Mrs. Easterberg.'

'When was that in relation to her death?'

'He left about ten days before.'

'Why did he leave?'

Mr. Macready jumped to his feet in objection.

'Can this witness answer that?'

'Oh, I know why he left', Miss Chatt began helpfully. 'Mrs. Easterberg . . .'

'Would you be quiet a moment please, madam', Mr. Macready said sternly. Turning to the bench he went on, 'I apprehend, your worships, that this witness was about to give hearsay evidence.'

All eyes came back to Paul Steadman, who was standing impassively waiting to proceed.

'Perhaps if my friend had given me a little more time, we'd have found out the source of the witness's knowledge', he said smoothly. 'May I now go on?' He looked towards Miss Chatt. 'Do you know the reason for the accused leaving Mrs. Easterberg's service as a result of what he himself told you or of what Mrs. Easterberg told you?'

'Mrs. Easterberg told me she was sacking . . .'

'Really!' Mr. Macready was out of his seat like a space rocket.

'You mustn't tell us what Mrs. Easterberg said to you', Steadman went on patiently, pretending to ignore the interruption. 'Did Lucas himself ever tell you why he was going?'

'No.'

'There!' Mr. Macready said, triumphantly eyeing Mr. Talbot and the justices.

Steadman blinked mildly at the ceiling. 'So you can't tell us why he left, Miss Chatt? Can't tell us of your own knowledge, that is? You only know from what Mrs. Easterberg told you, is that right?'

'And what I heard her tell him.'

'And what was that?' His tone was wheedling and he cast Macready a sly look.

'Mrs. Easterberg found him upstairs coming out of one of the bedrooms . . .'

'Was the witness there too?' This time Macready's tone was bored.

'Yes. I was dusting Mrs. Easterberg's room, and came out on to the landing when I heard their voices.'

'How did the accused react when Mrs. Easterberg gave him notice?' Steadman asked.

'He looked . . . well, he looked rather upset.'

'Angry?'

'Really, that's too bad!' Macready was on his feet again. 'Putting words into the witness's mouth like that.'

Heads switched back to Paul Steadman, who said unabashed, 'Well, how did he react, Miss Chatt?'

'Well, he did look just a little bit annoyed perhaps . . .'

'The answer would be more convincing if you hadn't suggested it', Mr. Macready muttered crossly.

Steadman said, 'I now want to ask you some questions, Miss Chatt, about the day of Mrs. Easterberg's death. It was a Wednesday, you'll remember.'

Miss Chatt pulled her hat more firmly on to her head and nodded.

'Your day off, I believe?'

'That is right.'

'What time did you leave the house that day?'

'A few minutes before half-past nine.'

'And how did you leave?'

'In my little car.'

'And where did you go?'

'I drove up to London.'

'And when you left the house who was in it?'

'Only Mrs. Easterberg.'

'She was alone?'

'Yes, quite alone.'

'In what part of the house was she when you departed?'

'She was sitting at her desk in the drawing-room writing out a cheque.'

There followed a pause in which Miss Chatt swallowed hard and Steadman thoughtfully turned the papers before him. Looking up, he said, 'I suppose you knew Mrs. Easterberg's habits fairly well through living in the same house and being her companion, didn't you, Miss Chatt?'

'Our relationship was strictly one of employer and employee', Miss Chatt replied primly.

'Quite. But I wonder if you can help the court about this. Where used Mrs. Easterberg to keep her money?'

Miss Chatt flushed with embarrassment. 'I hope you don't think I used to pry . . . I mean she kept her affairs very much to herself. Captain Corby can probably tell you better than I can about those sort of things.'

'I think you may have misunderstood me, Miss Chatt', Steadman said with a disarming smile. 'I was referring to cash about the house. Where used she to keep that?'

'Oh yes, yes, of course. She kept some in her brown handbag and some in her black handbag.'

'About how much would she normally have around the house?'

'Oh, I couldn't tell you that', Miss Chatt replied with a nervous smile.

'I don't mean an exact amount, of course. But about how much?'

'Quite a lot.'

'That's relative, Miss Chatt. What you call a lot, someone else might call very little. Five pounds? Ten pounds? Fifty pounds?'

'Oh, I think she usually used to keep between ten and twenty pounds in her handbags.'

'In each?'

'There was usually money in each.'

'Ten or twenty pounds in each of the bags, do you mean?' Mr. Talbot broke in. Miss Chatt nodded with the air of one anxious to please.

Turning towards a side table on which various articles in polythene bags were laid out, Paul Steadman said, 'Look at that cushion a moment, would you, Miss Chatt? Do you recognize it?'

'Yes, it's the one from the chair in Mrs. Easterberg's bedroom.'

'And that poker?' He indicated a two-foot length of steel with a hexagonal brass knob on one end.

'It's the poker from the grate in her bedroom.'

'I'd like to see those two articles', Macready said.

'They'll be exhibits four and five', Mr. Talbot interposed.

The cushion and poker were passed across to Macready, who examined them with a stern frown, first pummelling the cushion and then making a number of vicious chopping movements with the poker.

This created a stir of interest in which Dave Lucas himself joined. Then thrusting out his legs, he folded his arms across his chest, yawned and fell into contemplation of the raftered ceiling. It was the most boring day he had endured for a long time. In fact not since he'd been at school had he been forced to sit quiet for so long while others talked. And to think that for the past couple of weeks, he'd been looking forward to this day and to the change of scene it would provide. But now he almost wished he were back in Brixton prison. At least there he could talk and move around a bit. Without thinking, he started to whistle softly, but received a quick jab from the police officer at his side.

Meanwhile Paul Steadman had sat down and Macready had got to his feet. For several seconds he stared at Miss Chatt with fierce concentration, so that she passed her tongue nervously over her lips and fidgeted with her gloves.

'Was Mrs. Easterberg a somewhat overbearing person?' he suddenly shot out at her.

'Well, er . . . yes, I suppose she was what you might call a strong personality.'

'A determined old lady?'

'Well, ye-es.' Miss Chatt looked unhappily round the court as though she expected such *lèse-majesté* to be punished.

'And physically tough too?'

'For her age, she was remarkably well preserved.'

'How tall was she?'

Miss Chatt's mouth fell open in surprise. 'I . . . I'm afraid I can't answer that . . . I . . . "

Macready swung round and motioned Lucas to stand up.

'Was she taller than the accused?'

'Oh, yes.'

Fixing the witness with his sternest look, Macready said, 'After he had been given the sack did the accused ever display the slightest sign of animosity towards Mrs. Easterberg?'

'No; he just looked a bit upset, as I said.'

'He never threatened her?'

'Oh, no.'

'Never hinted anything about trying to get his own back?'

'Certainly not.'

'Never, in fact, said or did anything to make you think he would seek any kind of revenge?'

'Oh no, nothing like that at all.'

Macready had rapped out his questions with military forthrightness and he now sat down again, discarding Miss Chatt like a squeezed orange.

After her evidence had been read back to her and she had signed it, she retired gratefully to a seat just behind the dock and composed herself by busying herself with the contents of her handbag. The small flat bottle of cheap Eau de Cologne; the return rail ticket from London where she was now lodging in a dingy room at her cousin's house; the neatly folded white handkerchief; and the three pounds and ten shillings which had somehow got to last her till the end of the month. It was several minutes before her nose ceased twitching like a rabbit's and she felt sufficiently calm to be able to gaze about her.

She found Lewis Spicer smiling at her with what she took to be secret amusement and looked stiffly the other way. At least she still had her respectability, which was more than a lot of people could say for themselves! And fancy coming to court wearing a bright pink tie! She looked at the back of Dave Lucas's head and a small lump came into her throat. She felt there was a kind of bond between them; a bond of common experience. She secretly hoped he would get off: a feeling she would not have entertained if Lewis Spicer or Bob Pringle had occupied the dock.

By this time Sam Shoe, the postman, was in the witness-box and had answered Paul Steadman's preliminary questions.

'So you think it was about five minutes to ten when you arrived at Five Meadows Chase that morning?'

'That's right, sir', Shoe said cheerfully. 'Must have been just about then.'

'And what did you do when you got there?'

'What I said to the police in my statement you got in front of you, sir.'

'I'm afraid you must tell us again, Mr. Shoe. The court doesn't know what you said to the police on a previous occasion.'

Sam Shoe shrugged as if to disclaim all responsibility for the law's repetitious ways.

'Well, I rang and knocked like I said, 'cos I had this registered letter for Miss Chatt.'

'And was there any answer?'

'No, there wasn't', he replied, with studied forbearance. 'The whole place was as quiet as the grave.'

'You didn't see anyone at all?'

'Not a living soul, sir.'

'And what did you do?'

'Same as I told the police. I dropped what I had through the box and brought the registered away again.'

'And you didn't see anyone on your way down the drive?'

'No one, sir, and that's the truth.'

'In the past, when you've rung the doorbell, have you usually received an answer?'

'Always, sir. I've never known no one not to come before. It was usually Miss Chatt or Mrs. Winters.'

'Mrs. Easterberg ever?'

'Yes, the old lady too on occasions.'

'And on the day we're talking about you think that if anyone had been in the house, they could have heard you?'

Sam Shoe chuckled.

'Couldn't have failed to, sir. Normally someone'd come after I'd knocked and rung once. That morning I did it more'n once, I can tell you.'

Steadman nodded slowly to himself and sank back in his seat.

'No questions', Mr. Macready snapped, without looking up.

Sam Shoe listened intently while his deposition was read back to him.

'Yes, that's the gospel truth, sir', he said, when Mr. Talbot invited him to sign it, which he did with pains-taking deliberation and departed to take a seat next to Miss Chatt.

A minute later, bracing himself to meet the uncertain hazards presented by his next witness, Paul Steadman said, 'Call Ajit Singh.'

The interpreter bustled into court, turning to snap his

fingers at Ajit Singh like an angry diner trying to attract the attention of a half-witted waiter. Then Superintendent Blaker stepped forward and placed an enormous tome on the ledge of the witness-box.

'It's their holy book', he muttered at Paul Steadman as he returned to his seat. 'As soon as he's taken the oath, I've promised to return it, as they require it in another court this afternoon. It's the only copy for miles around.'

Meanwhile the interpreter was turning the pages of the book as though contemplating its purchase.

'Let the witness be sworn', Mr. Talbot said.

All that happened, however, was that Ajit Singh bent his head and whispered for several seconds in the interpreter's ear. The interpreter pursed his lips in apparent distaste at what he heard; then turning to the justices, he said, 'Ajit cannot take the oath on this book.'

'Why not? What's wrong with it?' Mr. Talbot asked.

'He may not touch it today', the interpreter replied enigmatically.

'What do you *mean*?'

'He's unclean today.'

'Unclean!' Mr. Talbot's voice rang with astonishment.

'He have intercourse with woman last night and therefore not yet clean and not able to touch the holy book.'

Mr. Talbot gave Paul Steadman a nonplussed look and said in an accusing tone, 'He's your witness, Mr. Steadman. What do you propose doing?'

Steadman sighed and addressed himself directly to the interpreter. 'Tell him that rule doesn't apply here. Tell him, too, that the consequences of refusing to be sworn will be infinitely worse.'

'I tell him', said the interpreter grimly, turning back to the witness and proceeding to harangue him fiercely for at least a minute. Ajit Singh said nothing but hung his head in glum silence. 'He's now willing to bare his conscience and tell the truth on the book', the interpreter declared at the end.

'I didn't know that the D.P.P.'s staff included spiritual advice amongst their accomplishments', Macready murmured sardonically.

Ajit Singh now placed a hand on the book and swore to tell the truth, the whole truth and nothing but the truth and Paul Steadman began his examination-in-chief.

'Is your name Ajit Singh?'

This formal question sent the interpreter into a lengthy discourse, at the end of which Ajit Singh made clicking noises with his tongue.

'Yes, he says his name is Ajit Singh', the interpreter declared with pride.

'Where do you live?'

Another colloquy followed before the answer came back.

'At the farm.'

Paul Steadman sighed. 'Which farm?'

'The farm the other side of the dead lady's house.' This time the interpreter replied without any reference to the witness at all.

Steadman pretended not to notice the omission and went on quickly, 'Do you know the accused?' With growing impatience he listened to an exchange of bitter-sounding words his question seemed to evoke. 'The answer is either yes or no', he broke in testily.

'No', retorted the interpreter promptly.

A gleeful smile lit up James Macready's face as Paul Steadman silently counted up to ten before continuing.

'Is the witness saying he has never seen the accused man before?'

'He see him several many times.'

'Well, why did he say "no" to my last question?'

'It is simple, sair', the interpreter said in a patronizing tone. 'Ajit not *know* the accused, like I don't *know* you, sair; but he has seen him many times in the village.'

'How much of this is what the witness has said and how much the interpreter's own brand of gloss?' Macready observed at large.

But Steadman took no notice.

'When did he last see him in the village?' he asked.

An age seemed to pass before the reply came back.

'On the day of the bloody murder', the interpreter announced complacently.

This inevitably provoked giggles amongst the spectators, but Paul Steadman was too relieved to notice. He bestowed rewarding smiles on witness and interpreter. From then on Ajit Singh's evidence flowed with relative smoothness and accorded with what he had told the police. When he finished his questioning, he sat down limply and watched Macready rise to cross-examine.

'How much English can the witness speak?' Macready asked in a brisk tone.

'A few small words only,' the interpreter replied after another voluble exchange with the witness, which was also accompanied by graphic gestures.

'And understand?'

'He understand a little better than he speak.'

At this point, Dave Lucas leant over the front of the dock to attract his advocate's attention. Macready turned his head and they held a short, whispered conversation.

'You don't like the accused, do you, Singh?' he asked a few seconds later, glaring in the direction of the witness.

It really looked as though, this time, the interpreter and Ajit Singh were going to come to blows. Each appeared to hold himself back with the utmost difficulty during the searing exchange of words which ensued. Eventually the interpreter said stolidly, 'He say it not true that he don't like him.'

'Is he saying then that he does like him?' Macready asked belligerently.

With a resigned shrug, the interpreter turned back to the witness and, after a surprisingly short and docile discussion, said, 'Yes, he quite like him.'

Macready nodded grimly. 'Isn't it a fact,' he asked, 'that the accused once warned the witness against foisting his unwanted attentions on Miss Gawler?'

'Please?' the interpreter said uncomprehendingly.

At this point, Mr. Talbot broke in. 'Wouldn't it be better, Mr. Macready, if you phrased your questions in direct speech, as though the interpreter didn't exist.'

'I wish he didn't', Macready muttered sourly beneath his breath. Looking up, he said loudly and with a trace of annoyance, 'Isn't it true that the accused spoke to you about pestering Miss Gawler? Told you not to bother her?'

The interpreter received the question impassively and proceeded to translate.

'Ajit say that not true', he, in due course, replied laconically.

'Do you remember the accused saying he'd knock your block off—strike you, that is—if you didn't leave Miss Gawler alone?'

'Ajit think Miss Gawler very nice girl,' the interpreter said, 'but he never interfere with her.'

'Interfere in the dictionary or in the Sunday newspaper sense?' Paul Steadman murmured with quiet malice.

'I suggest,' Macready said severely, 'that you never saw the accused at all on the morning of the murder and that you have made it up out of revenge.'

'You want me to translate?' the interpreter asked wearily.

'Naturally.'

This forensic suggestion of Mr. Macready's, however, had the surprising effect of sending Ajit Singh into giggles, in which the interpreter showed an inclination to join.

'The witness take your suggestion seriously, he not amused', he remarked.

With an exhausted sigh, Macready sat down.

'Just like trying to stir thick treacle', he observed to Paul Steadman.

Meanwhile Mr. Talbot began the infinitely tedious task of reading the witness's deposition back to him via, once more, the interpreter.

Dave Lucas rubbed his chin and absentmindedly picked at a small pimple. He wondered when Jean would be called to give evidence and exactly what she would say. From the letters which she had written to him in prison, she appeared to think they would soon be together again. She spoke of his predicament and of the various court proceedings as though they were no worse than a nasty cold in the head. And this wasn't callousness, but a refusal, even an inability perhaps, to face possible consequences. But he, Dave Lucas, faced them all right. He'd been in trouble with the law before in his young life and knew more than to expect a good fairy to wave her wand. Though he couldn't be bothered to follow the evidence all the time, he knew the police had built a substantial case against him and that he was going to have to fight hard. It would be a dirty fight too. The police didn't like it when a prisoner refused to make any incriminating admissions, especially when it was someone like himself whom they regarded as rightly belonging behind bars. It was always his sort they picked on for the frame-ups.

Manton and Yates didn't seem a bad couple, but that wouldn't prevent them trying to improve upon the evidence. At any rate, that was Dave Lucas's opinion as he prepared himself to rebut the case which the prosecution were making against him. It was like being a fly caught in a spider's web. For much of the time you lay quiet, almost lifeless; then suddenly you'd put all you had into the chosen moment of struggle. And if you were lucky, you got free. If not, it was just too bad.

And like the fly, Dave Lucas had a limited horizon: his needs, simple, physical and of the moment.

In a small room outside the court sat Richard Corby and Jean Gawler, awaiting their turn to be called as witnesses.

Corby's expression was nervous and strained and he constantly fidgeted with his wrist-watch. Jean, however, sat quite still, as she played a game with herself counting the wood blocks in the plain uncarpeted floor.

Corby looked across at her through half-closed eyes. She must be an unimaginative child to be so composed, he thought. After all, hers was the most dramatic testimony of all of them in a way; certainly it had the best press value. For some time the urge to talk had been growing within him. He shuffled his feet noisily to attract her attention and then as she looked up, he said with a quick, nervous smile:

'They're taking a long time with that Indian chap, aren't they?'

The girl shuddered. 'He gives me the creeps.'

'I was in India during the war, so I'm used to them', he remarked conversationally. But Jean didn't appear to be very interested, so he went on, 'I'm sorry you've got dragged into this, Jean. I'm afraid it's not a very pleasant experience for anyone.'

The girl looked at him with a faintly perplexed expression.

'I'm sorry about Mrs. Easterberg too', she said diffidently, as though unsure whether this was a proper reply.

Corby fingered his black tie. 'Have you got anywhere you can go away to afterwards? Any aunts and uncles you can go and stay with?'

'I've got an auntie in Kent', she replied, puzzled.

'Perhaps your father can fix up for you to go and visit her.'

'But I don't think Mum and Dad want me to go away.'

'Probably better if you did for a while. Help you to forget and that sort of thing.'

'Forget? Do you mean . . .' The sentence trailed away as she stared at him incredulously.

Corby swallowed uncomfortably.

'I was just thinking it might be best for you.'

'Of course, you *believe* he's done it, don't you?' she said, the thought striking her with apparent suddenness. He was about to reply when she went on, 'I *know* he's innocent. Dave wouldn't hurt anyone. It wasn't him who killed her, sir.'

Corby studied her for several seconds without saying anything. Then he said, 'Don't pin too many hopes on him, Jean, or you may get hurt.'

The girl bit her lip.

'That's what the police told me. But I know he'll get justice; I know they'll see that he didn't do it.'

Her invocation of 'justice' and of 'they' nettled Corby, and he retorted acidly, 'If Lucas didn't do it, I don't know who did.'

'Oh, lots of people might have', she said, and then a moment later added, 'I'm terribly sorry, sir. I didn't mean it like that.'

'Like what?'

'Well, that there were lots of people who wanted to kill Mrs. Easterberg.'

'I'm glad of that anyway', he said stiffly. 'Although, apart from yourself, nobody has any doubt that this was the work of a burglar—of a young thug.'

Jean's cheeks coloured at his tone.

'I can think of several people in the village who might have done it to look that way.'

'You'll be laughed out of court if you make wild suggestions of that nature', he remarked sternly.

It was, perhaps, fortunate that at that moment the door opened and a police officer said, 'Captain Corby? This way please, sir.'

Corby followed him into court, aware that his feelings had been tiresomely ruffled by his conversation with Jean. He entered the witness-box and inclined his head stiffly at the justices before taking the oath in the tones of one determined to give each word its solemn recognition. As he put the Testament down, he let his gaze go round the court. This was the moment chosen by Bob Pringle to make his entry. He came through the door which led to the public seats and stood for several seconds impassively surveying the scene. Corby looked quickly away. Even at that distance he thought he could feel the power of the man, like a blast of air from an open oven. He hated him now for the dominion he had exercised over his aunt. Indeed, he was almost ready to believe Pringle possessed hypnotic powers, that he was the reincarnation of some evil spirit. His feelings, as he secretly acknowledged, were a measure of his own hurt vanity.

Holding his head erect, Corby determined that the man should get no inkling of how much his presence disconcerted him. Soon, anyway, he was caught up in answering Paul Steadman's questions.

'On this particular day,' Steadman was saying, 'did you go to your aunt's house on your own initiative or as a result of something that had been said to you?'

Corby smiled indulgently. He had once begun to read for the Bar and knew something about leading questions and hearsay evidence. Or believed he did. His smile was accordingly intended to convey to Paul Steadman that he was a member of the same secret society and so perfectly at home in legal circumlocution.

'My aunt had telephoned me that morning . . ."

'Yes, I follow', Steadman cut in quickly.

'And asked me to . . .'

'You mustn't tell us what she said to you, Captain Corby.'

Corby looked pained. 'I'm sorry', he said primly. 'I thought you asked me . . .'

'No, you've answered my question. The reason you went to her house that afternoon was as a result of something she said to you over the telephone the same morning.'

'Yes, as I was going to explain. She particularly . . .'

This time there was an indignant chorus of protest and Corby relapsed into sulky silence. He was quite sure he remembered some rule which permitted what a deceased person had said to be given in evidence.

Steadman went on imperturbably. 'And what time did you arrive at the house?'

'It must have been around five minutes to five.'

'And by which door did you enter?'

'The front door.'

'Was it locked?'

'No, it never was in the daytime.'

'And what was the first thing you noticed?'

'A letter on the mat.'

'Did that surprise you?'

'Yes, because there's no afternoon delivery in Five Meadows and I knew it must have been there since morning.'

'So what did you do?'

'I called out my aunt's name.'

'Was there any reply?'

'None.'

'Then what?'

'I went to try and find her. Actually, I picked up the letter first and saw that it was one addressed to my aunt, which made me more worried.'

'In what way?'

'Well, she wasn't likely to have left her own mail lying on the mat, but . . . er . . . well, she might have conceivably left it there if she'd seen it was for . . . for someone else.'

Mr. Macready scribbled furiously in his notebook and put a couple of x's in the margin beside what he had written.

'And in due course you went to her bedroom?' Steadman said, piloting the witness through well-charted waters.

'Yes.'

'And there you found your aunt?'

'I did.' Corby lowered his head and stared with a strained expression at the ledge of the witness-box.

'Just look at the album of photographs: number six, if you'd be so good.'

'Yes', Corby said, doing as requested.

'Does that photograph fairly depict the scene as you found it when you entered your aunt's bedroom?'

'Yes, as far as I remember, she was lying as shown in the photograph.'

'On the floor, face down in that cushion, that is?'

'Yes.'

'Just look a moment at the poker, exhibit five. Did you see that in the room?'

'It was lying on the floor not far from my aunt's body.'

There followed a few more questions and then Paul Steadman sat down.

Mr. Smalley whispered to his two colleagues and peered over his desk at the top of Mr. Talbot's head.

'Mr. Talbot', he hissed. 'We'd like to adjourn for a few minutes.'

Mr. Talbot got up and after a short whispered confabulation announced, 'The court will adjourn for ten minutes.' He turned towards the witness. 'I must ask you not to speak to anyone, Captain Corby, as you're still giving your evidence. At least, I assume Mr. Macready will want to ask you some questions in cross-examination.'

'Indeed I will', Macready remarked crisply.

'Then perhaps you'd be so good as to remain in court and not mix with anyone', Mr. Talbot said.

Corby nodded, and went and sat by himself on a hard chair against the wall.

'Hello, Bob, coming out for a smoke?' Lewis Spicer asked, as he and Pringle pushed their way through the crowd.

'You been in court the whole time, Mr. Spicer?'

'Yes. Thought I might get an article out of it. Not a court reporter's piece, I don't mean. Something more off-beat. Cameo portraits of some of the witnesses, perhaps.'

'Like that bit you wrote about our village, you mean?'

Spicer laughed. 'Poor old Mrs. E. I never thought anyone could become so upset over one silly article.'

'I reckon she got her own back though, Mr. Spicer.'

Spicer gave Pringle a sharp glance, but found himself confronted by a fathomless expression.

'From what I hear, her death hasn't done you any harm', he observed, with a glint in his eyes.

'I don't know what you've been hearing, do I?' Pringle said stolidly, filling his pipe.

'That she's left you quite a bit of money, Bob. In fact that in many ways you've come off better than the gallant captain.'

'Some people talk too much.'

Spicer laughed again. 'It's nothing to what they'll soon be doing when her will is made public.'

Pringle grunted a reply and moved away from Lewis Spicer's side. Suddenly he turned back and, in a tone at once unemphatic yet mandatory, said, 'Don't start putting me or my affairs into any of your articles, Mr. Spicer.'

Then, turning sharply on his heel, he pushed past a small knot of people and went and stood alone on the pavement outside the courtroom's main entrance.

'How's it going, sir?' Manton had asked Paul Steadman as he emerged to stretch his legs for a few minutes.

'All right, I think.'

'Witnesses O.K.?'

'Yes, they've all more or less come up to proof so far.'

'Including Ajit Singh?'

'Yes, his evidence wasn't seriously shaken.'

'But I can tell that you've still got reservations about the case', Manton remarked, searching Steadman's face.

Steadman sighed. 'Well, not really. Certainly not to the point of believing we're prosecuting the wrong chap. It's just that I find it difficult to reconcile certain features.'

'The trouble with you lawyers, sir, is that you always want all the evidence to fit together neatly. You're reluctant to accept that, human nature being what it is, practically every case must have untidy ends sticking out.' The two men were silent for several seconds. Then Manton asked, 'Mr. Macready cross-examining much?'

'A certain amount, but he's not wasting time. In view of the defence that Lucas isn't the person who committed the crime, there isn't a great deal he can ask many of the witnesses.'

Manton shook his head reflectively. 'Thank heavens for that footprint. It's enough to hang him by itself.'

'Ready to continue, Mr. Steadman', a voice called out, and Paul Steadman retraced his steps into court, bumping as he did so into Dave Lucas, who was standing in the doorway with his escort, exhaling a last lungful of cigarette smoke.

Lucas pulled aside with a muttered 'Sorry' and then grinned at the police officer beside him. Through a crack in the door opposite, he caught a sudden glimpse of Jean sitting alone in the witnesses' waiting-room and made as if to take a closer look.

'Go on, back into court', the officer said gruffly.

'How much longer for?'

'They'll adjourn for lunch at one.'

'Tell the cook I'll have treacle pudding for mine', Lucas said cheerfully.

'You're too fat as it is.'

'It's not fat. It's muscle.'

'Muscle wrapped up in treacle pudding if you ask me', the officer retorted, obviously pleased with his repartee. He gave Dave Lucas a prod, just as Superintendent Blaker scowled at them through the doorway and barked, 'Hurry up and bring the prisoner in.'

Lucas gave him a pitying look as he made his way back inside.

The justices resumed their places and Corby stepped back into the witness-box to face Mr. Macready, who, brushing a lock of hair off his forehead, rose to cross-examine him.

'You've told the court, Captain Corby, that you went up to your aunt's house on this Wednesday evening as a result of her having phoned you in the morning.'

'Yes, that's right.'

'What exactly did she say to you on the phone?'

'Oh, come now, surely we can't have that', Paul Steadman said in a tone of sweet reasonableness. 'It's pure hearsay.'

'But the witness is under cross-examination', Mr. Talbot replied, anxiously.

'Quite true, sir, but I know of no rule of evidence which says that hearsay is admissible when adduced in cross-examination.'

At this point, Macready himself intervened.

'I agree with my friend that the rule is the same for both sides. But'—and here his tone became coaxing—'I do suggest that in practice, courts often permit the defence to adduce hearsay evidence of this nature in fairness to the accused.' He let this sink in; then went on, 'After all, your worships, this young man is charged with murder and it would be terrible indeed if his defence were to be hampered by a too rigid application of a rule, which, as we all know, is frequently relaxed in an accused's favour.'

'Really!' Paul Steadman expostulated. 'My friend has no right to drag emotion into this. The rules of evidence are designed to ensure that a man receives a fair trial and that justice is achieved. They're not there to be unilaterally disregarded simply because the defence wish it.'

'Relaxed, not disregarded', Macready commented.

Both advocates were now on their feet, addressing the justices like competitive salesmen.

'Hearsay evidence is frequently admitted if the defence want it, isn't it?' Mr. Talbot said, in a troubled tone.

'Particularly when it's something relevant said by the deceased person in a homicide case', Macready added quickly.

'How do you know that this is relevant?' Steadman asked sharply.

'I just think it will be', Macready replied.

Silence fell and the two lawyers sat down again. Mr. Talbot stood up and held a whispered conversation with the justices, who bent their heads together. After a while, Mr. Smalley, the chairman, said, 'We'll hear the witness's answer first and then decide whether it should be recorded in his deposition.'

'Judgment of Solomon', Macready murmured.

'Wildly improper', rejoined Paul Steadman.

Macready now turned back to the witness.

'Well, Captain Corby, tell us what she said to you over the phone.'

'She just asked me to look in about teatime.'

'Did she say why she wished to see you?'

'She said it was something important.'

'Yes, but did she say what it was?'

'I got the impression that something had gone wrong.'

'You got that impression from what she told you?'

'Yes.'

'But she didn't say what had gone wrong?'

'No, not in so many words.'

'What exactly do you mean by that?'

'Well, I gathered . . .'

'How much more of this guesswork and surmise are we to have?' Paul Steadman inquired witheringly.

'Yes, I really think we must draw the line somewhere, Mr. Macready', Mr. Talbot observed anxiously.

'If you please, sir', Macready said, in a tone much too sweet for Steadman's liking. 'I won't pursue this particular matter any farther. Perhaps we could just have on the deposition, "I went to the house at my aunt's urgent request since she told me something had gone wrong and she had an important matter to discuss with me".' He looked at Steadman. 'Do you agree that that is what the witness said?'

'I never heard him use the word "urgent". Otherwise it accords with my recollection of what he said.'

Macready nodded with satisfaction. 'I'm much obliged.' He was well pleased with himself. He had succeeded in establishing that there was something untoward in the Easterberg *ménage* on the morning of the murder. Something unknown and mysterious with which, in due course, to distract and beguile a jury. He turned back to the witness.

'Would it be fair to say, Captain Corby, that your aunt was a person of strong likes and dislikes?'

'Yes, I suppose it would.'

'And I assume that you'd agree with me that she might have made enemies as a result of holding strong views about things and people.'

'I'm not aware of her having had any enemies', Corby replied stiffly.

'No, please don't misunderstand me: I'm not naming individuals; merely citing a possibility. A possibility which arises from her strong reaction to people.'

'I suppose that everything's possible. But all I can say is that I don't know of any enemies my aunt might have had.' Corby paused and added, 'Certainly no one who might have wanted to murder her.'

Steadman looked at Mr. Talbot to make sure he was recording this postscript by the witness. He was beginning to weary of the hares put up by his opponent. Of course, they were all an indication of the thin material Macready had to work with, though that didn't make the chase after them any less exasperating.

Macready was halfway to sitting down when he suddenly straightened and said to the witness, 'Oh, just one last question, Captain Corby. Would I be right in saying that your aunt's favourite colour was blue?'

'As a matter of fact you would', Corby replied, with the air of someone acknowledging the sudden materialization of a conjurer's rabbit.

Steadman and Mr. Talbot exchanged mystified looks, before Mr. Talbot asked, 'Do you want that written down?'

'Certainly', Macready replied in his crisp voice, affecting unawareness at the curiosity his question had aroused.

While Corby's deposition was being read over to him, Superintendent Blaker, who, since he was not being called as a witness, had remained in court, stepped over to Paul Steadman's side and whispered loudly in his ear:

'The old girl's strong likes and dislikes are both in court.' Observing Steadman's puzzled expression, he added with a suppressed belly laugh, 'Pringle and Spicer.'

Corby signed his deposition and went and sat next to Miss Chatt in the seats behind the dock. She gave him a fleeting smile as she made room for him and then leaned forward intently, cupping her chin in her hand to listen to the pathologist's evidence.

Dr. Innes' appearance in a magistrates' court invariably created the same sort of extravagant interest as Sir Laurence Olivier's might if he had suddenly decided to take part in a performance by a village dramatic society.

He had performed tens of thousands of autopsies and given evidence in hundreds of trials, including a large number of headline-hitting murder cases.

He had the appearance of a well-groomed bank manager and was numbered as a friend by the great in many diverse walks of life.

Unlike many medical men who are called upon to give evidence but who are unpractised in the art, he had the knack of making his testimony comprehensible to laymen and was also aware of the various legal issues involved. Thus, when Paul Steadman gave him the cue concerning the blow on the deceased's head he said, flicking his eye down to the open notes before him, 'It was a blow of relatively minor severity, which caused a superficial laceration at the back of head, but which did no damage to the underlying structures.'

'What exactly do you mean when you say "relatively", Dr. Innes?'

'I mean that though it was sufficient to have stunned the deceased woman and rendered her unconscious, it had not fractured the skull or caused damage to the brain, as very often occurs in these cases.' He gave the justices the engaging look of one whose only aim was to assist them. 'Quite clearly, your worships, that poker, exhibit five, is the type of weapon with which a person's skull could be severely fractured. The fact that this didn't happen in this case indicates that the degree of force used was relatively mild.'

'But sufficient to cause unconsciousness?' Steadman put in quickly.

'Oh, certainly, yes.'

'Do you associate the head injury with the cause of death?'

'Medically, no. The cause of death was asphyxia due to

suffocation. The deceased had lain face downwards in the cushion and been suffocated.'

'Can you say what her condition must have been at that time?'

'Oh, she must have been unconscious. A healthy adult, as the deceased was, couldn't have become suffocated in this way unless she were unconscious.'

'So that if she had not been knocked on the head with the poker in the first place, she wouldn't have died?'

'That follows, though it's scarcely a medical proposition', Dr. Innes observed with a faint smile.

'What can you tell the court about the cushion which was the actual cause of her death?'

The cushion was handed to the witness, who studied it gravely before replying.

'It is a particularly soft cushion and the deceased's face caused a deep indentation in its surface. In fact I found particles of material in the deceased's breathing passages which appeared to have come from the outer surface of the cushion.'

'How long must she have lain with her face in it before she died?'

'A matter of a minute perhaps.'

'Are you able to say whether the dent in the cushion was more consistent with her having fallen face downwards into it or with the cushion having been put under her head subsequently?'

'I don't think that I can answer that with any real assurance. Close to the laceration at the back of the head, however, I did find a bruise which was of the sort one finds when someone falls down and bangs their head against a hard, flat surface, such as a floor. Unlike the laceration, it had not in my view been made by the poker.'

He looked up from his notes. 'I think that's as far as I can help you over that.'

There followed further questions to elicit more precise details of the findings of the witness in relation to the cause of death. Then Paul Steadman sat down and all eyes turned on Macready.

He rose slowly to his feet, looked towards the doctor with one slightly raised eyebrow and said, 'Cross-examination of this witness is reserved.'

Dr. Innes' expression was one of mild amusement as he turned to listen to his deposition being read over. After he had signed it, he was bound over to attend the court of trial and was then released by the justices to go about his business. With friendly nods all round, he departed.

Mr. Talbot looked at his watch and went into consultation with the justices.

'Is your next witness a long one?' he asked Paul Steadman over his shoulder.

'It's Dr. Renshaw from the laboratory.'

Mr. Talbot made a face and turned back to consult further with Mr. Smalley and his colleagues. When he resumed his seat, he said, 'All right, Mr. Steadman, call your witness and we'll see how it goes. The justices have decided to adjourn at one o'clock.'

Dr. Renshaw took the oath with an air of perfunctoriness and opened a large orange folder before him, then, hitching one leg round the other, he looked at Paul Steadman to indicate he was ready for the first question.

For several minutes, however, his evidence consisted of his enumerating the various articles and samples which he had examined and specifying the source from which they had been received. It is always one of the vital necessities of laboratory evidence that each examined item is carefully traced from its point of origin to the scientific expert who attends court in order to talk about it.

This done, Paul Steadman said, 'Tell us first, Dr. Renshaw, about your examination of the poker, exhibit five.'

'The poker, exhibit five,' intoned the witness, 'is made of steel and weighs approximately two and half pounds. At one end of it, I found smears of human blood of Group O and adhering to the blood two human head hairs. These hairs are identical in structure to those in the sample of the deceased's hair, exhibit twelve.'

'What group is the deceased's blood sample, exhibit eleven?'

'Also Group O.'

'Tell us now what you found on examination of the cushion, exhibit four.'

'The cushion is square, being two feet by two feet. It is well filled with feathers. On one side, I found stains of saliva such as might have come from the deceased person's mouth if she lay with her face buried in it.' Dr. Renshaw looked up from his notes. 'I also found some smears of blood of Group O. These were on the opposite side of the cushion to the salival stains and appeared to have come from a small amount of blood which was on the floor beneath the cushion.'

'Or vice versa perhaps?'

'No, I think the blood on the cushion came from the floor and not the other way about.'

'Ye-es', Paul Steadman said thoughtfully, studying the report which Dr. Renshaw had submitted and deciding how much of it was strictly relevant to the prosecution's case. 'I think we come now to the accused's clothing which you examined, and in particular to his trousers. What can you tell the court about those?'

'In the turn-ups of the trousers, exhibit thirteen, I found debris, part of which consisted of particles of pampas grass. This was identical with the pampas grass which had been in a vase in the deceased's bedroom and which I saw scattered on the bedroom floor when I visited the scene.'

Paul Steadman gave the justices significant looks to ensure that they appreciated the importance of this piece of evidence. It was one further strand in the rope which tied the accused to the scene of the crime. While Mr. Talbot was still writing the evidence down, he looked quickly round to see if Lucas was displaying any reaction to the proceedings, but was disconcerted to be stared back at as though he were a Peeping Tom.

In fact, Dave Lucas had been listening attentively to Dr. Renshaw's evidence and had only that moment directed a look of surly distaste at the back of Paul Steadman's head.

'Is there much more of this witness?' asked Mr. Talbot, laying down his pen and massaging his fingers.

'Very little', Steadman replied in a comforting tone. Turning to the witness, he went on, 'I want you now, Dr. Renshaw, to tell us about the accused's shoes, exhibit fourteen.'

The witness leaned over the edge of the witness box rather like a giraffe bending its neck to feed and picked up a pair of black shoes which had thick crêpe soles.

'I have examined these shoes, your worships, and have compared the soles with the plaster cast, exhibit fifteen, which is the cast of a footprint found in a flower-bed beneath the deceased's bedroom windows. As a result, I formed the opinion that the print of which this is the cast was made by the left shoe of this pair.' Picking up the plaster cast in one hand and the left shoe in the other, he continued, 'Let me demonstrate.' This he proceeded to do, holding both high up in the air for all to see. 'The ridges in the cast agree exactly with those on the bottom of the shoe.' He gazed about him with the sardonic air of one who is slightly bored with his own miracles.

While attention was still riveted on the witness, Paul Steadman sat down.

'Any questions, Mr. Macready?' Mr. Talbot asked, a trifle impatiently. It was getting on for the luncheon adjournment and his stomach was beginning to make protesting sounds.

'I'd just like to have a look at the exhibits to which the witness has referred', Macready said, ignoring the clerk's hint.

With a studious air, he held up each of the articles about which Dr. Renshaw had given evidence, while everyone watched him. Finally he put them all down save the shoe, across whose sole he passed his hand with a furrowed expression. He seemed to be on the point of asking a question, but said instead, 'On second thoughts, I propose to reserve cross-examination of this witness.'

'Gamesmanship!' Blaker muttered disgustedly in Paul Steadman's ear. 'Bet he hasn't a question in mind. Just trying to make us think he's got all sorts of clever tricks up his sleeve. If you ask me, Dr. Renshaw's just about sewn Master Lucas up in his shroud.'

The witness, who had listened to his deposition being read over to him with the air of a thoughtful pelican, now unwound his legs and came forward to sign it, after which Mr. Smalley announced, 'The court will adjourn till two o'clock.'

In the general hubbub of dispersal which ensued, Manton felt a slight pluck at his sleeve as he stood in the passage outside the courtroom. He turned to find Jean's eyes anxiously scanning his face.

'May I see him, please?' she asked in an eager whisper.

'Not now, Jean. You've got to give evidence this afternoon, it wouldn't be right', he replied not unkindly.

'When it's all over, may I see him then?'

Manton became paternal. 'It depends on what the court says, Jean.'

'If I'm allowed to visit him in prison, I don't see why I shouldn't see him here', she observed with a pout.

'Because it wouldn't look good if the prosecution's witnesses were seen talking to the accused just before they gave their evidence. You might lay yourself open to all sorts of suggestions.'

It was clear, however, that she found his explanation unsatisfactory, and she turned away with an expression of defiance.

Macready, meanwhile, had hurried out after Dave Lucas to confer with him in a police cell under P.C. Green's discreet observation.

Lucas was patently worried and could hardly wait to light the cigarette which he accepted from his solicitor. Macready eyed him thoughtfully, then said, 'I decided it'd be best not to cross-examine the pathologist or laboratory witness at this stage. It's clear that the prosecution have got a *prima facie* case against you and so there's no point in disclosing our various lines of attack until we reach trial. Good thing to keep the other side guessing', he added encouragingly. Lucas nodded, but his solicitor got the impression that he had hardly been listening. 'Anything you want to ask me before I go off and get a bite of food?'

'That bit that last bloke said about my shoe having made the footprint in the flower-bed. What about that?'

'They say it was made by your shoe: you say it couldn't have been because you weren't there. That's right, isn't it?' Lucas nodded, as though hypnotized by his solicitor's bland assurance. 'Don't let that worry you too much then. Where did you buy those shoes, by the way?'

Lucas named a large multiple store and Macready nodded with satisfaction. 'Anything else on your mind?' he asked, noticing that Lucas still appeared troubled. 'Don't bother about all that scientific evidence. It's not as damning as it sounds and we'll be able to do things with it when the time comes. I shall be busy between now and your trial searching for ammunition with which to shoot at all those witnesses. I've already got quite a little store.' He got up and stuffed his papers underneath his arm. 'I know it's apt to be depressing when you hear the prosecution present their case and very little is done on your side. But I warned you what today would be like and you mustn't let it get you down. One of the objects of these proceedings—*the* object in fact—is to tell us exactly what we've got to face at the trial and so to enable us to prepare your defence.'

His short pep-talk finished, Macready gave his young client a bright smile of encouragement. 'See you back in court this afternoon', he said, and departed.

Dave Lucas started to eat his own food slowly and mechanically. He scarcely tasted it, however.

His solicitor, for all his well-meaning advice, had said nothing to help solve the problem which beset him, and he was suddenly filled with an overwhelming sense of loneliness. So much so that his eyes began to prickle with tears of self-pity.

He was still lost in the hopeless maze of his thoughts when P.C. Green unlocked the cell door and took him back into court for the afternoon session.

NINE

THE press men in court watched with eagle-eyed interest as Jean Gawler made her way to the witness-box. Here was their most promising source of a good eye-jerking headline.

They were not disappointed, for on her arrival in the box, she immediately turned and gave Dave Lucas a quick smile of devoted love, which he acknowledged with a wrinkle of the nose.

'Take the testament in your right hand and read out loud the words on the card in front of you', Mr. Talbot intoned, without looking in her direction.

Paul Steadman, who had been rearranging his papers, became suddenly aware of the silence which followed the clerk's instruction. On looking up he noticed that Jean was standing quite still and making no move to take the oath. At that moment her eyes met his and she said, 'I don't want to give evidence.'

'I'm afraid you must', Steadman replied politely but firmly.

'Supposing I refuse to say anything.'

'The court would be forced, though doubtless with great reluctance, to hold you in contempt. To commit you to prison, in fact.'

Jean bit her lip and cast her eyes down at the ledge of the witness-box. Mr. Smalley, the chairman of the justices, leant forward and spoke.

'Now take the oath, Miss Gawler, and let's get on with the case.'

Reluctantly lifting the testament as though it were made of lead, she proceeded to mumble the words of the oath, keeping her eyes fixed on the floor.

Paul Steadman had very few questions to ask her and most of them innocuous at that. It was obvious from the expression of surprise on her face when he sat down that she had expected something far more gruelling.

'How long have you known the accused?' Macready asked as his first question.

'Since he first came to Five Meadows.'

'That would be about three months ago, would it?' Jean nodded. 'And you're very fond of him, aren't you?'

'Yes.' Her voice was scarcely above a whisper.

'So fond of him that you would be willing to tell lies to help him?'

'I haven't told lies.'

'But would you if you thought it would help him?'

'I only want to tell the truth. I don't know any lies which will help him.'

'If you please, Miss Gawler', Macready observed in a smoothly forensic tone. He went on, 'Has Lucas always been good to you?'

'Yes, very.'

'Gentle and kind?'

'Yes, always.'

'Have you ever known him be violent?'

'No, never.'

'Did he ever mention Mrs. Easterberg to you when he was working for her?'

'Yes, he did.'

'What did he say about her?'

'He said she was a nice lady.'

'Did he say how he liked her?'

'He said he did like her.'

'How many times did you see him after he had left Mrs. Easterberg's employ?'

'Only once.'

'When was that?'

'About a week later.'

'Where?'

'In London.'

'You went up to London and met him by arrangement, do you mean?'

'Yes.'

'Did he mention Five Meadows at all on that occasion?'

'He said he never wanted to come here again.'

'Why was that?'

'Because he was upset at the way he'd been treated.'

'When you say *upset*,' Macready asked quickly, 'do you mean he was angry and wanted revenge?'

'No, it wasn't that way at all', Jean said, suddenly scared lest anyone might draw a wrong conclusion.

'Did he mention his plans to you on that occasion?'

'Yes, he wanted to get a job on a liner.'

'Did he say anything at all about returning to Five Meadows to commit a burglary?'

'No, nothing like that. He never wanted to come here again.'

'Did you see him in Five Meadows on the day of Mrs. Easterberg's murder?'

'No.'

'If he had come here that day, do you think he'd have got in touch with you?'

'I'm sure he would.'

As Mr. Macready sat down, Jean gave Lucas a flickering smile.

'Just one or two matters in re-examination', Paul Steadman murmured, rising to his feet. 'Everything you've told the court about the accused's character is based on a mere three months' acquaintanceship, is it not?'

Mr. Macready was immediately on his feet. 'I hope my friend is not seeking to discredit his own witness. That question sounded to me to be thinly-veiled cross-examination, rather than re-examination. Indeed, I can think of nothing I asked the witness which would require my friend to re-examine at all.'

'My friend must forgive me if I decline to take any lessons in advocacy from him', Steadman remarked tartly. 'I submit my question was a perfectly proper one.'

The two advocates glowered and Mr. Talbot sniffed as though at a disagreeable odour. Turning to the witness he snapped, 'Is it right you've only known the accused for three months?'

Jean nodded with a look of dumb unhappiness, and Steadman went on, 'What was your reaction, Miss Gawler, when the accused told you he was proposing to get a job on a liner?'

'I don't know what you mean.'

'Well, were you pleased at the idea?'

'No.' She scarcely spoke above a whisper, but there was no one in court for whom the small monosyllable did not convey a page of meaning, did not conjure up a scene of tearful pleading.

'And I suppose you tried to dissuade him?'

'I asked him not to go.'

'Quite; and he agreed?'

'He said he'd think it over.'

'And that was the last time you saw him until you joined him in London, is that right?'

'Yes.'

'Thank you, Miss Gawler.'

On vacating the witness-box, Jean selected a seat by herself at the back of the court. As she sat down, however, Miss Chatt came tiptoeing across to her.

'Feeling all right, Jean?' she asked kindly. 'Don't worry dear, you said nothing to let him down.' Jean smiled at her gratefully and allowed Miss Chatt to take her hand in hers and pat it soothingly, as they watched Manton take the oath in the carefully articulated tones which police officers habitually use in the witness-box.

His evidence-in-chief was short and related largely to the finding and arrest of the accused. When it came to cross-examination, Mr. Macready, speaking in tones of great emphasis, said, 'It's a fact, is it not, Superintendent, that from first to last the accused has denied having had anything to do with the crime?'

'That is so', Manton replied equably.

'Has told you that he was miles away at the time?'

'He told me he was in London the whole of that day.'

'Well, that's miles away, isn't it?' Macready snapped.

'You made it sound rather more than the twenty miles or so that lie between London and here, sir.'

Macready snorted scornfully and sat down.

The last witness of all was P.C. Green. He stood in the box like a blue missile and directed his evidence in stentorian tones at the wall opposite to him. When he reached the final full stop, Macready announced that he had no questions to put in cross-examination. As soon as his deposition had been read over and signed, Paul Steadman got up and said, 'That completes the evidence for the prosecution upon this charge and I ask for a committal for trial.'

'Have you any submissions to make, Mr. Macready?' Mr. Talbot asked.

'No, I concede that there's a case to answer.'

'Big of him', Superintendent Blaker muttered in Manton's ear.

'The question of the court of trial now arises', Mr. Talbot went on. 'The next assizes for this county are not for another four months.'

'I ask that the case should be sent for trial at the Old Bailey. The next session of that court opens in three weeks' time', said Macready.

'What have you to say about that, Mr. Steadman?' Mr. Talbot asked.

'I have no observations to make in the circumstances. It's a matter entirely for the court.'

Mr. Smalley and his colleagues went into a flurry of whispering, after which Mr. Smalley said, 'We find there is a *prima facie* case and shall commit the accused for trial at the next session of the Old Bailey.'

'The Central Criminal Court, that is', Mr. Talbot added, in a schoolmasterish tone.

Five minutes later, with all formalities completed, the justices bowed and departed, and Dave Lucas was led away to the cells to await his return to Brixton prison and three more quiescent weeks.

Turning to Paul Steadman, Macready said with a smile, 'I don't know whether he did it or whether he didn't; but I do know that for once it isn't all your way.'

TEN

'HOW'D the case go yesterday?' Tom Coles asked, coming into Paul Steadman's room and flopping into a chair.

'He was committed to the Old Bailey.'

'I saw that much in the papers. Have any difficulty with it?'

'No-o. Not yet.'

'But you're expecting some, eh?'

Paul Steadman screwed up his face and nodded.

'I'm certain we've got the right fellow in the dock,' he said, 'but the evidence isn't as strong as I could wish. It's one of those cases where a skilful defence will be able to wear away a bit here and a bit there until there isn't much left of the original edifice.'

Coles gave a short laugh. 'Trouble with you, Paul, is that you've got so used to prosecuting cases in which the evidence is one hundred per cent unchallengeable that you begin to shiver in doubt when it's anything less.'

'It's not just that there are gaps in this evidence, Tom, but I'm not even happy that we're drawing the right deductions from what there is.'

'What makes you say that?'

'An occasional surreptitious glance in court at the accused himself. You know how it is, you're propounding some piece of evidence and suggesting what inference should be drawn from it when you suddenly happen to notice the accused's expression and realize that you're right off beam at that point.'

'Yes, but it's usually over the non-essentials. I remember once doing a terrific piece of reconstruction all about how from various fingermarks found on a window, the accused must have climbed into a house that way. After the case was all over and the chap had got five years he told the police he'd walked in through the front door using a skeleton key. His fingerprints had got on to the window when he'd opened it to release a large moth.

'That happened because he denied having ever been inside the house; there was no evidence to show anyone had entered by the door, but there were his fingerprints on this window and moreover he didn't shut it properly afterwards, so that it looked as if that had been his means of entry. But the point is that he'd been inside the house all right and my false deduction had no bearing on his guilt.' Coles paused, noticed Steadman's still doubtful expression and went on, 'Your scientific evidence, Paul, plants Lucas fairly and squarely at the scene of the crime and I don't see what else you've got to worry about. Just because you suggest he removed the money from her purse before he killed her when it may have been after; or that he held the poker in his right hand when it may have been his left, doesn't make a ha'porth of difference. The thing is he obviously did it. If prisoners choose not to make confessions, they must expect a few inaccuracies in the reconstruction of their crimes.'

Paul Steadman burst out laughing, not so much at Coles' words as at the genuinely heartfelt tone in which he uttered them.

'I expect you're right, Tom, and anyway it's now someone else's worry. Nevertheless, I should like to know why he departed from the house in such a hurry as to leap out of the bedroom window.'

'Perhaps because he heard someone downstairs.'

'There wasn't anyone in the house.'

'One of the daily helps.'

'They weren't there. One was on holiday, the other was looking after her sick child and the companion was out. The house was empty apart from Mrs. Easterberg herself. After all, that's one of the points we've made against this chap. That he knew she'd be the only person in at that hour of the morning.'

'The postman then', Coles said, rather in the tone of a parent trying to assuage its progeny's fanciful doubts. 'Maybe he heard the postman.'

'Yes, I hadn't thought of that . . .'

'There you are then! Except that the probable explanation is that he jumped out of the window in sheer unreasoning panic. You should know better than try and rationalize human conduct, Paul.' Coles stifled a yawn. 'How's Jane? Still writing?'

'Yes', Steadman replied gloomily. 'A story about a colony of animated vegetables. You wouldn't believe what she has them do, but it means that for the moment we're practically living on fish, meat and bread as she can scarcely bring herself to boil a brussels sprout, or peel a potato even, for fear of a literary trauma.'

Coles got up, stretched and said with a grin, 'I must go back to my case of the choirmaster who embezzled the new church organ funds.'

'How very untypical', Steadman observed dryly, as his friend raised a hand in mock farewell and made to leave.

Unclipping his pen, Paul Steadman reached for a sheet of paper and started to draft his observations to counsel in the case of the Queen against David Lucas.

The Attorney-General had nominated Mr. Freebody, Q.C., and Mr. Smythe to conduct the prosecution at the Old Bailey, and, to Steadman's relief, both counsel were happily free of tiresome idiosyncrasies.

He always found difficulty in making his friends understand why he and his colleagues in the Director of Public Prosecutions' department took their cases no farther than the magistrates' court and why the prosecution at the court of trial was entrusted to counsel outside the department, who had in fact been nominated specifically for the occasion.

'But you're a barrister, Paul, I don't understand why you don't handle the case all the way through', they would say in tones of incomprehension.

'It's because we're a government department and, in the eyes of the law, we're equated with a solicitor's office. And solicitors mayn't appear at assizes in the role of advocate', he would explain patiently.

But he was not even sure that his wife, Jane, really understood the position. She just accepted it, in the same way that she accepted electricity and the internal combustion engine.

By far the busiest person in the days which ensued was Lucas's solicitor, James Macready. For him work proper only started with his client's committal for trial, since that was the first occasion the strength and weaknesses of the prosecution's case became known to him. Now that the prosecution's evidence had been deployed, he was able to start preparing the defence.

Lucas's defence was, of course, simple. It was, 'I didn't do it. I wasn't there. I know nothing about it.' It was necessary, however, to see where these short, staccato denials could be buttressed by other evidence; evidence which would support his client's word and chip away, if possible, the testimony of Paul Steadman's witnesses.

Two days after the committal, Macready visited Lucas in prison and spent an hour and a half with him. It was not until he had left and called on his way home at an address in Bermondsey that he knew it had been a fruitful visit. In a street not far from Borough underground station he parked his car and rapped on the door of an end terrace house.

'Is Mr. Leonard Bernie in?' he asked the suspicious, sharp-eyed looking youth who opened it.

'Who wants him?'

Mr. Macready handed over one of his cards. The youth studied it and his expression became more suspicious; hostile even.

'What do you want?'

'My business is with Mr. Bernie', Macready replied with dignity.

The youth frowned. 'Wait', he said slowly, and shut the door hard in Macready's face. When, a couple of minutes later, he opened it again, the solicitor was forestalled from voicing some of his own views by the youth's altered expression.

'I thought your name was kind of familiar. You're the bloke who's defending Dave Lucas.' He said it as a statement of fact. 'I just checked it *was* you in the paper. Come in.' He turned to lead the way down a dingy passage. 'I'm Lennie Bernie', he said over his shoulder as Macready followed him, not without hesitation.

Half an hour later when Macready left, he was feeling distinctly pleased; was even prepared to recognize that Lennie Bernie's original suspicion of him was quite understandable in the circumstances.

The next morning, after half an hour spent in his office

to deal with the mail, he set off for Five Meadows and a talk with Bob Pringle.

He drove into the village past the courthouse, whose thick outer door was now shut fast, through the main street and on to Bob Pringle's garage, where he swung off the road and parked on the newly cemented forecourt. The petrol pumps, the metal rack with the containers of oil, the watering can even, all looked so very new and eager to be used.

When he got out of his car, he found Pringle staring at him in thoughtful silence from the entrance to the workshop.

' 'Morning', Macready called out amicably. But there was no response, and he walked over to where Pringle was standing. 'My name's Macready—James Macready. I'm . . .'

'I know who you are.' Pringle's tone was not encouraging.

'Well, that saves a lot of bother. You'll know then, Mr. Pringle, why I've come to see you.'

'Will I?'

'It's about my client, Lucas. You weren't called as a witness for the prosecution and I've come to see if you know anything which might help the defence.'

'I don't.'

Macready managed a short laugh. 'Have you any objection to my talking to you for five minutes or so to satisfy myself about that?'

'I've got nothing to tell you', Pringle repeated flatly.

'Won't you give me the opportunity of finding that out for myself?'

'There's no point. I'm busy, I imagine you're busy, so why waste time?'

Macready's eyes hardened and he said sternly, 'Lucas

is on a capital charge, Mr. Pringle, and if he's convicted of it, he'll almost certainly be hanged. It's my job to dig up every bit of evidence I can that might assist his defence, and'—here his tone took on a note of faint menace—'the law can deal effectively with anyone who withholds vital information in such a case.'

To his surprise, Pringle gave a loud laugh, then said abruptly, 'Don't waste your time mouthing idle threats at me. I don't know anything which'll help get young Lucas out of his fix, just as I don't know anything which'll put him in it worse.' He appeared to be filled with sudden indecision; then curiosity getting the upper hand, he asked, 'Any particular reason for your thinking I could help you?'

'You apparently knew Mrs. Easterberg very well and . . .'

'Oh, just that', he broke in. 'Well, if you want to know, I told her young Lucas was a dishonest little reformatory boy and she'd regret ever giving him a helping hand.'

Pringle turned on his heel to go, when Macready, stung by his tone, retorted coldly, 'I hope that she never regretted giving *you* a helping hand, Mr. Pringle.'

Pringle looked back, chin thrust out, his expression hard and glinting. But he said nothing and, a second later, Macready found himself alone. Still riled at the ungraciousness of his reception, he walked briskly back to his car, got in and drove out into the road with protesting sounds from engine and tyres. His mood was not helped by the fact that, for the moment, there seemed to be nothing more he could do so far as Pringle was concerned. You couldn't subpoena a witness without knowing what he was going to say and you couldn't force him into telling you something he didn't wish to. Maybe Pringle didn't know anything which could assist the defence, but James

Macready dearly wished for an opportunity of twisting his tail to find this out.

He was still burning with annoyance when he pulled up outside Lewis Spicer's colour plate cottage and gave the ancient bell-chain a vigorous tug.

Spicer himself opened the door.

'Why, it's Mr. Macready of the law', he exclaimed sardonically. 'Come on in. I've been longing for an excuse to stop writing. In fact I'd just made up my mind to break off anyway and have a cup of coffee.' He led the way into a low-ceilinged room which ran the depth of the cottage and looked something like a contemporary stage set for a writer's den.

At one end was a small desk with a portable typewriter and sheaves of pale blue paper scattered around.

'This used to be two rooms, of course', Spicer said, as Macready looked about him with polite interest. 'But I had the dividing wall removed and use it as a combined study and living-room.'

Macready's gaze took in the walls, which were adorned with a number of modern landscapes—at least that was what he took them to be. 'I imagine you must have had a good deal done to make it as charming as it is', he said with a quick smile.

'Yes, and I thought I'd never get the workmen out of the place. They took three months longer than they estimated. But it was worth it in the end. I'm blissful here.' All the while he spoke his eyes never left Macready's face. 'Let me just show you the rest of it before we get down to business. At least, I take it you have come on business.'

'Yes, about . . .'

'Dave Lucas? I imagined so. Here, come and have a look at my kitchen.'

This was followed by a tour of the upstairs region

which included an inspection of Spicer's own bedroom where a huge expanse of divan, complete with pink nylon sheets and pillow slips, practically covered the floor space, and of the bathroom, which had a fitted carpet of old gold, an all black bath and gold coloured fittings.

'It's charming', Macready said uneasily, as they went downstairs again. As a straightforward, healthy young man whose own standards of domestic comfort were the casual ones acquired at school, he was oppressed by Lewis Spicer's obviously meticulous thought for every detail of his home. Leaving him alone in the living-room, Spicer disappeared into the kitchen to fetch the coffee.

He returned shortly, bearing a large silver tray with two cups and a silver coffee pot and sugar bowl on it.

'I hate nasty, cheap things, don't you?' he asked, as he carefully placed the tray on a small glass-topped table. 'Some people, I know, could live in a pigsty and not even notice, but I've always liked nice things.'

He poured the coffee out, handed a cup to Macready and held out the bowl of coloured crystal sugar. 'Very gay, isn't it? So much nicer than the ordinary white lumps that look like Eskimo bricks.'

For a few seconds there was silence as each sipped at his coffee. Then, again fixing Macready with eyes that glinted shrewdly behind his spectacles, he said, 'What is it you want to know about Dave Lucas?'

'I want to know whether you can assist the defence in any way, Mr. Spicer.'

Spicer sighed. 'I'd have got in touch with you if I could. I'd like to help. I'd like to very much. He looks a nice boy and I'm sorry he's got mixed up in this.'

Macready sharpened his ears.

'Mixed up? You think then that there's more to it than has appeared on the surface?'

Spicer scratched the end of his nose. 'No-o. That wasn't exactly what I meant.' He raised his eyes to Macready's and lowered them again. 'I just meant that I'm always sorry to see young men in trouble. If you tell me some way in which I can help him get out of it, I'll willingly do so.'

'Did you know my client quite well?'

'I didn't know him at all, unfortunately. Of course I'd seen him about and smiled at him, but I don't think I've ever spoken to him in my life.'

Macready found himself blushing.

'Oh, I . . . er . . . must have . . . er . . . misunderstood', he stammered. 'I had an idea you knew him and I was going to ask you whether he'd ever said anything to you about Mrs. Easterberg.'

Spicer shook his head sadly. 'I'm afraid not.' Then in a brighter tone he added, 'Of course Bob Pringle had a wonderful motive for murdering the old termagant. Why can't you build up a subtle defence suggesting it was he?' His eyes shone with sardonic amusement and Macready wondered how far Spicer intended that the suggestion should be taken seriously.

'One doesn't build up a defence, as you put it, without having a foundation of evidence', he replied a trifle tartly, after a pause.

'But I thought that was your current expedition, a search for evidence.'

'It is, and it's not being very successful, Mr. Spicer.' He rose. 'Thank you for the coffee and for giving me some of your time, but I mustn't keep you away from your typewriter any longer.' He looked meaningly towards the cluttered top of the desk.

Again Spicer's eyes roamed intently over his face. He said, 'I really am sorry I can't help you more, but I wish you all the luck with the case. I shall follow it with the utmost interest and keep my fingers crossed for your client's acquittal.'

'Thank you.' James Macready's voice held a note of polite surprise. He walked down the short garden path to his car. As he turned it round to drive back in the direction of Pringle's garage, Spicer waved to him gaily from the cottage doorway.

He's obviously a queer, Macready thought, and they're often enough unpredictable, untrue even to their own form. Not so much immoral as amoral. But the question was whether he was anything more than he appeared. Macready shrugged off his thoughts and turned up the drive which led to Five Meadows Chase.

A hundred yards or so before he reached the house, he parked the car and, climbing over an iron railing, strode across the meadow which flanked the drive. From time to time he stopped, examined the ground and changed his course.

By the time he regained his car, he had covered the meadow and the bank of a stream on its far side with the zeal of a terrier.

Whistling with quiet thoughtfulness, he got in and drove back into the village. There, he made calls on a number of further people, from whom he hoped he might be able to glean something helpful to the defence. But he learnt nothing of consequence and about lunchtime he returned to his office.

It seemed that there was no one in Five Meadows who could, or would, come to Lucas's aid.

The next step was to deliver to counsel his brief for the defence.

ELEVEN

Two days later, Manton and Sergeant Yates set out for Five Meadows by car.

Since Lucas had been committed for trial, they had attended a number of conferences with Paul Steadman and with the two counsel who had been appointed to conduct the prosecution at the Old Bailey. It was as a result of the last of these conferences that they were making their present journey.

It was that relatively rare thing, a glorious English summer's day and the countryside, once they were free of the outer suburbs, had the look which made you want to immerse yourself in its lushness.

'Hope this weather holds when I go on leave', Sergeant Yates remarked, as he turned off the main road into the lane which led to the village.

'When are you going?' Manton asked lazily.

'End of July. Almost as soon as the trial's over.'

'Where?'

'Cornwall this year. My wife's cousin runs a guest house near Falmouth and they've offered to put us up. Mind you, we've got to pay, but it'll be a cut price. Looking forward to some fishing; my eldest boy's real keen on it. I believe he'd go fishing in our goldfish pond if there was nothing else.'

A quarter of an hour later, the car pulled up outside the Corbys' house, a styleless structure built in the inter-war period.

'Mrs. Corby?' Manton asked, when a woman opened the front door to them. She had a faintly petulant expression and a long upper lip which, he judged, would be quick to pucker in disapproval.

'Yes. But I don't think I know . . .' She let the sentence trail away.

'My name's Manton. Detective Superintendent Manton of Scotland Yard. This is Detective Sergeant Yates.'

'Oh, of course, you want to see my husband. If you come in, I'll go and fetch him. He's at the back somewhere.'

Manton had noticed half a dozen glasshouses in a field at the rear of the house. Showing them into a small front room which looked unused and smelt strongly of furniture cream, Linda Corby firmly closed the door on them and went off to find her husband.

'Wouldn't care to be married to her', Yates observed agreeably. 'Like going to bed with a cold hot-water bottle.'

Before Manton had time to reply, the door opened again and Corby, followed by his wife, came in.

'Good morning, Superintendent', he said, without warmth. 'What is it now?'

'We're just trying to close a few gaps in the evidence', Manton replied with a placating smile. 'One or two small points which have cropped up in conference and which the D.P.P. has asked us to see you about.'

'I should have thought Mr. Steadman would have got in touch with us direct', Linda Corby broke in, with a sniff. 'After all, his wife and I are friends.'

'Oh, these things are always dealt with through the proper channels, Mrs. Corby. The D.P.P. never has direct contact with witnesses, apart from expert ones.' Spreading out his hands in a gesture of disarming frankness, he went on, 'One always tries to foresee what the defence will put up and to block off any bolt holes.'

'Surely this young ruffian hasn't got the beginnings of a defence, has he?' Corby exclaimed. 'I know juries can be pretty stupid, but they'd have to be worse than that before they could acquit Lucas of this charge.'

'Oh, we've got a strong case all right, but it's still prudent to leave nothing to chance. Hence our visit.'

'Go ahead, then, Superintendent. Let's hear what's brought you.'

'This business of your aunt phoning you on the morning she was murdered, Captain Corby. Counsel wonder whether you can cast any more light on it. They want to prevent the defence dragging it in as a red herring.' Observing Corby's expression of cold surprise, he continued, 'The fewer the red herrings, the better. Juries are apt to manufacture enough of their own anyway. Counsel wondered whether, after further reflection, you could suggest what it might have been that caused your aunt to telephone that morning.'

Corby shook his head curtly.

'Can't help you.'

His wife leaned forward. 'I wouldn't be surprised if it wasn't because she'd spotted Lucas lurking around somewhere.'

Manton nodded slowly, as though to indicate she had made a good point. 'It doesn't quite tie in, does it, Mrs. Corby, with her asking your husband to come and see her that afternoon? Also, there'd surely have been no reason for her not telling him why she was calling if it had been as you suggest.'

'Huh! You didn't know my husband's Aunt Sophie. She enjoyed making unnecessary mysteries. I still believe that her call had to do with Lucas.'

Manton looked towards Corby for agreement or dissent. He said in a coaxing tone, 'If by any chance Mrs. Corby's theory is right, it's important we should try to prove it.' Then, after a slight pause, he added with a sigh, 'Though I confess that I don't see how we ever can.'

Corby studied the lighted end of his cigarette with a thoughtful expression for several seconds.

'Personally,' he said, looking up at Manton, 'my own belief is that she wanted to speak to me about Pringle. I confess that didn't occur to me at the time, because I had no idea then of the extent to which he had her under his influence. I knew, of course, that she used to ask his opinion and advice on all manner of things, which one wouldn't normally consult one's garage man about. I even suspected that she lent him money for his business; but the terms of her will came as a complete surprise and showed how far she'd allowed herself to fall under his spell.' There was a pinched, drawn look about his face, and he obviously spoke with considerable emotion.

'Your guess may well be right, Captain Corby, but of course even if it is, it doesn't follow that the call had any bearing on her murder.'

'Precisely, and that's why I don't see how counsel expect to get any further with the point. My guesses aren't going to help them demolish a red herring. Though I repeat that I can't for the life of me see how my aunt's phone call can really give rise to such.'

A few minutes later, Manton and Yates got up to go. Linda Corby bade them a formal farewell at the front door, but her husband accompanied them out to their car.

'I'm sure you'll be glad, Captain Corby, when the trial's over', Manton remarked as they shook hands.

'I shall, but of course not even Lucas's conviction and despatch from this earth will end the matter. It's not so much the murder itself as the shadows it has cast which have caused such distasteful publicity. And that, I'm afraid, is bound to linger for quite a while. It's inevitable in a village community like this.'

Manton nodded understandingly.

'I suppose it's the old story of the pebble in the pond and the ripples which continue long after the pebble has sunk to the bottom and disappeared', he said.

Looking past them into limitless distance, Corby remarked with surprising vehemence, 'Lucas may be the product of the times, of a social malaise, of a broken home and the rest of it, but there is a limit to society's patience with these young ruffians, and nobody's going to tell me that his extermination won't have a salutary effect on others.'

'I gather that you're in favour of capital punishment', Manton said with a wry smile.

'For the likes of him; yes, I am.'

As they drove away, Yates turned to Manton. 'Sounded to me, sir, as though the Captain wanted Lucas's head on a charger not so much for murdering his aunt as for stirring up a muck heap.'

'Mmm', Manton replied, nodding vacantly.

On the day before Lucas's trial opened at the Old Bailey, Jean Gawler visited him in Brixton prison and Miss Chatt had her hair done.

Jean had, in fact, been going to the prison twice a week. On this, the last occasion, she left as she had done on practically each of the previous ones, troubled and anxious. She wanted to believe that the change which had come over Dave Lucas was no more than one would expect to see in someone awaiting trial for murder. But she couldn't help recalling that it was only since his committal for trial that the change in him had become so marked. During his first spell in prison between arrest and the hearing in the magistrates' court he had been no different from usual.

But now he appeared withdrawn, listless and in a permanent state of morose detachment. She had done her best to cheer him up, had made it clear that she, at any rate, would never lose faith in him, but all her efforts to revive his buoyant spirits had been unavailing. At the most, she would receive a flicker of an abstracted smile and a monosyllabic response.

Each time she had tried to find out what was on his mind, whether indeed there was anything in addition to the obvious strain of awaiting trial, he had denied that anything particular was amiss and would say, without conviction, that he would probably be brighter next time she came. But he never was.

On this last afternoon Jean had whispered across to him, 'It won't be long now, darling.'

'Mmm?' he had replied, obviously recalling his thoughts with difficulty.

'Not long before we're together again.'

To this he had said nothing, but his perplexed and troubled expression had caused her heart to miss a beat.

'You have liked my coming to see you, haven't you, Dave?' she had asked, her eyes hopefully searching his face for a sign of the old gaiety and fun she thought she remembered.

'Sure, sure', he had replied dully.

Soon after this, the visit had ended and with a heavy heart she made her way to the bus stop. But at least it couldn't last much longer. By this time next week, he would have been acquitted and she would be able to be with him again. The alternative Jean steadfastly refused to consider.

Although Beryl, the girl who always attended to Miss Chatt's hair, had not seen her since the day of the murder, she had basked luxuriantly in the reflected glory of having a client involved in a notorious murder case.

'Oh, I've been thinking of you and your dreadful experience so much of late', she began, as soon as Miss Chatt had surrendered herself and was in the chair. 'Of course, I read all about your evidence in the papers. To think it was the day you sat in this very chair that your poor employer was murdered: that she was lying dead on her bedroom floor all the time you were sitting here', she continued with morbid relish. Miss Chatt decided to stay silent and let her run on. 'Lying there with her head battered in by that burglar. It's terrible the way some people have to die, isn't it? Of course, you having been a nurse wouldn't be so shocked as someone like me. If it'd been me that had found her . . .'

'But I didn't find her', Miss Chatt said, in mild reproof.

'No, of course, it was her nephew, wasn't it, that Major somebody or other?'

'Captain Corby.'

'Yes, that's who I mean. Terrible for him it must have been. Suddenly to find his aunt murdered like that. Was he very fond of her?'

'Naturally.'

'The police acted quick, didn't they, getting that young teddy boy who'd done it?'

'Yes, they were most prompt', Miss Chatt remarked primly.

'And now you're going to give evidence at the Old Bailey!' Beryl stood back and thoughtfully inspected Miss

Chatt's head. 'I suppose you might get your picture in the papers too, mightn't you?' she asked, in a hopeful tone.

'I doubt it.'

For several minutes, Beryl prattled on about the Lucas case and then turned on to a big breach of promise case that was currently filling the pages of the evening papers and in which the younger son of an earl was being sued by the daughter of a bookmaker, who, it had just been revealed, was taking bets from his friends on the result.

Apart from the fact that she didn't know anyone connected with it, she obviously preferred it to the squalid crime in which Miss Chatt had become involved as a witness.

'I suppose he'll be hanged, won't he?' she said, suddenly returning to what she referred to as 'your case'.

'I hope not', Miss Chatt replied quietly.

'Don't you think he did it then?'

'All the evidence points to his having done it,' Miss Chatt explained carefully; 'but it's just that I hope he won't be executed. You see, I got to know him when he worked for Mrs. Easterberg and I formed rather a liking for him.'

Beryl shook her head in slow wonderment. 'To think you know a murderer, Miss Chatt. And not just one of your own family either.'

Miss Chatt allowed herself a faint smile at this unintentionally ambiguous observation. 'Did the police ever come and see *you*, by the way?' she asked suddenly.

'Me? No! no! What about, do you mean?'

'They questioned us all about our movements that day and I told them, of course, that I'd been here in the morning and I just wondered if they'd checked it with you.'

Beryl shook her head sadly. 'No, they never came.' She

brightened. 'Think! I might have been asked to give evidence too.'

Miss Chatt smiled indulgently, and the girl went on, 'I could have told them how you couldn't have done it because you were sitting in this very chair.'

'Mrs. Easterberg was killed a good while before I got here. I'm afraid the police would hardly have regarded you as being able to provide me with a satisfactory alibi.'

'But you came earlier that morning. I remember quite well because I wasn't sure until you arrived whether you'd be able to make the earlier appointment.'

Miss Chatt laughed. 'All right, but I'm not looking for an alibi, you know. I'm not the one charged with the murder.'

'That Yard detective looked rather nice', Beryl said wistfully.

'Yes, he was.'

'Pity he never came.'

'It seems to me a pity that it was I and not you who got mixed up in this case, since you'd obviously have enjoyed it far more than I have.'

Beryl sighed her agreement, put the finishing touches to Miss Chatt's hair and reluctantly released her.

'There! I've made it look really nice. Now mind you don't go and hide yourself under a hat when you go to court.'

Miss Chatt promised that she wouldn't, also that she'd give the fullest account of her forthcoming experiences on her next visit, and departed.

TWELVE

NUMBER One court at the Old Bailey was as far removed from Five Meadows magistrates' court as a ducal mansion from a crofter's cottage.

As the minutes ticked by towards half-past ten, its rows of seats were filled with those who had come merely to watch and listen—they formed the majority—and, grouped together in the well of the court, those who were preparing to move into forensic battle. A sharp but civilized battle of words, in which one word alone might provide the key to a jury's verdict.

Paul Steadman sat at one end of the large, solid table which filled the well of the court. At the other was James Macready, looking scrubbed and full of nervous tension, as though he were about to go on trial himself. Behind them sat their respective counsel, wigged and gowned and outwardly relaxed.

The judge's clerk came through a door at the back of the bench, and smiled a greeting at them. On the judge's desk he placed, with fastidious care, a fat black notebook and beside it six sharply pointed pencils. Then, standing back, he cast a quick proprietory look over everything like a butler surveying the table he has laid. A final adjustment of the position of the carafe of water and he appeared satisfied. After a short, whispered conversation with the clerk of the court, he disappeared again through the door at the back.

A few minutes later, there was a series of sharp raps

on the door at the farther end of the bench and, as everyone stood up, Mr. Justice Gooch entered, attended by robed dignitaries of the City of London. In his left hand he carried a pair of white gloves, and an oblong of black material—the black cap which he would wear if Lucas was sentenced to death—and in his right a small posy of gay flowers.

He took his seat, disposed of the posy and other articles and sat back in the huge leather-backed chair at perfect ease. He was a new judge, only just fifty and looking younger, and his scarlet robes and white wig showed small sign of wear.

The clerk of the court stood on his seat to speak to him. When he turned back again, he said in a loud clear voice, 'Put up David Lucas.'

All eyes now turned to the immense dock which filled the centre of Number One court, as into it from the cells beneath came Dave Lucas, escorted by two prison warders. He stepped to the front and stood facing the judge across the table round which Steadman and Macready were still sorting their papers. Steadman watched him with relaxed interest.

He looked youthfully innocent and more than one female heart sighed and was filled with compassion as the clerk of the court read out the indictment.

'David Lucas, you stand indicted with capital murder, the particulars being that on the twenty-second day of May you did murder Sophie Easterberg in the course or furtherance of theft. How say you, are you guilty or not guilty?'

'Not guilty', Lucas said in a quiet, expressionless voice.

The clerk of the court now went on, 'Prisoner at the bar, the names that you are about to hear called are the names of the jurors who are to try you. If therefore you wish to object to them or to any of them, you must do so as they come to the Book to be sworn, and before they are sworn, and your objection shall be heard.' He turned to the jury box, where nine men and three women sat in varying degrees of apprehension. They stood up and an usher handed a Testament and printed card to the first. He took the oath, handed the Testament and card to his neighbour and sat down. Eventually all twelve had been sworn without objection and the clerk put Lucas formally in their charge. 'Members of the jury, the prisoner, David Lucas, stands indicted with capital murder, the particulars being that on the twenty-second day of May he murdered Sophie Easterberg in the course or furtherance of theft. To this indictment he has pleaded not guilty and it is your duty to hearken unto the evidence and to say whether he be guilty or not.'

The preliminaries were over and the clerk sat down. Mr. Justice Gooch motioned Lucas to be seated also. Then, looking towards prosecuting counsel, he said, 'Yes, Mr. Freebody.'

'We're off', Steadman thought to himself with a sigh, and leaned back in his chair to listen.

Mr. Freebody rose, hitched his gown more securely round his shoulders and began his opening speech.

'May it please your lordship. Members of the jury, in this case I appear for the crown with my learned friend, Mr. Smythe, and the prisoner is defended by my learned friends, Mr. Cleaver and Mr. Webley.'

It was not unlike the introduction of the panel in a television quiz and Steadman watched the jury's glance go from face to face along the row as the advocates' names were mentioned. Mr. Freebody paused impressively before continuing.

'Members of the jury, as you have heard, the prisoner

stands indicted with murder—with capital murder. As most of you probably know, parliament passed an Act in 1957 which had the effect of abolishing the death penalty except for certain classes of murder. Amongst these is murder committed in the course or furtherance of theft, which is what is alleged against this prisoner. I mention that to you since you have heard reference in the indictment to *capital* murder and might be wondering exactly what it meant in this context. Your charge is, of course, to say whether or not the crown has satisfied you of the prisoner's guilt; you are not concerned with penalties and must not let the question of penalty influence your verdict in any way. Your verdict must be based on evidence given in this court and on that alone.'

Mr. Freebody launched into a lucid explanation of the law applicable to this particular case, and concluded, 'Before you can bring in a verdict of guilty, therefore, the Crown must satisfy you beyond reasonable doubt that this young man Lucas killed Mrs. Easterberg, either intending to do so or at least intending to do her grievous bodily harm, and as to that you will remember that I've told you that in law every person is presumed to intend the natural and probable consequences of his acts. And that the killing occurred in the course or furtherance of theft. Now let us turn to the facts.'

For the next twenty minutes, Mr. Freebody particularized the evidence which the jury would shortly be hearing. With unimpassioned logic he marshalled the facts against Dave Lucas, holding each one up in its deadliest light for the jury to see. They for their part sat mesmerized by the performance. It was better than T.V., better than the cinema; in fact, it was the real thing.

At length Mr. Freebody approached the end of his opening. 'Although this prisoner has denied the charge throughout, you may think, members of the jury, that the evidence against him could scarcely be stronger had he indeed admitted this terrible crime. You will, of course, listen with great care to everything that may be said on his behalf; you will accept entirely and without question the direction which my lord will give you as to the law. But if at the end when you retire to consider your verdict, the Crown's evidence still stands unshaken, then the Crown says that it will be your duty to find this prisoner guilty of the charge brought against him. And now, with the assistance of my learned friend, I will call the evidence before you.'

Mr. Freebody sat down and the spell of silence broke as reporters hastened out of court to catch the early afternoon editions with their stories, and members of the public turned to whisper to their neighbours in the sudden release of tension. Paul Steadman twisted round to give counsel a smile of approbation.

An usher frowned heavily and, getting up, called for silence in a stern, commanding voice, at the same time raking the rows of seats with a forbidding glare.

So the morning wore on while the formal and uncontested witnesses followed each other into the witness-box. Dave Lucas sat alternately back on his hard chair with arms folded across his chest and eyes focused on his feet stuck straight out in front of him, or slumped forward with arms dangling aimlessly down between his legs so that only the top of his head could be seen. He would glance up as each new witness reached the box, but then, Paul Steadman noticed, he seemed once more to lose complete interest in his surroundings.

The first of the witnesses of substance to be called was Miss Chatt. She had heeded Beryl's admonition and was wearing a small hat which looked, however, a trifle ill at ease on a sea of springy curls.

Her examination-in-chief elicited the same evidence she had given before the magistrates and the cross-examination, for which she nervously braced herself, was the reverse of all she had expected. Not only was she not bullied, hectored and lured headlong into hideous lawyers' traps, but Mr. Cleaver gave every sign of trying to make her his friend for life.

Lewis Spicer, who had got himself into the seats reserved for V.I.P.s, watched her with amusement.

'Miss Chatt,' Mr. Cleaver said with a winning smile, 'is it fair to say that so far as you're concerned, the accused was always respectful?"

'Yes.'

'Hard-working?'

'Yes, he was.'

'Apparently keen to give satisfaction in his work?'

'Yes.'

'Do you know that Mrs. Easterberg was fond of him?'

'I don't know about fond.'

Mr. Cleaver smiled disarmingly. 'Perhaps that isn't quite the right word. May I say "That she liked him"?'

'Yes, I think she did, in her own sort of way.'

'What sort of way was that?' Mr. Justice Gooch asked in one of his rare interruptions, so that everyone suddenly looked towards him.

'She wasn't a demonstrative sort of person, you understand, sir', Miss Chatt explained.

The judge nodded and turned back to his notebook.

'And did he, the accused, appear to get on with Mrs. Easterberg?'

'Oh yes, until she gave him the sack.'

'Ah yes, I was just coming to that, Miss Chatt. After Mrs. Easterberg had given him notice to leave, did you ever hear him use any threats against her?'

'No, certainly not.'

'Or give any hint that he contemplated revenge?'

'No.'

'Did he, in fact, ever show that he bore any grudge against her?'

'No, I don't think so.'

Mr. Cleaver sat down and Mr. Freebody rose.

'Just one matter before you leave the box. You have been asked these questions about grudges and revenge, etcetera. Tell me, Miss Chatt, what was the interval of time between the deceased dismissing Lucas and his actual departure?'

'Well, actually it all happened in one day. She found him on the landing by her bedroom door one morning and he left immediately after lunch.'

'Thank you. So there wasn't much time for the expression of grudges. . . .'

Mr. Cleaver jumped to his feet. 'I hope my learned friend is not going to use re-examination as an excuse to comment on the evidence.'

But Mr. Freebody had meanwhile sat down and was casting a meaning look at the jury.

Paul Steadman smothered a yawn. So far no fireworks.

Next came Captain Corby, looking pale and martyred and wearing a heavily-knotted black tie. His evidence, too, was no different from that which he had given before the magistrates.

When Mr. Cleaver rose to cross-examine, the witness braced his shoulders, and firmly grasped the ledge of the box.

'Apart from your aunt's body lying on the floor, am I right in saying that the only sign of disorder in the bedroom was her notecase or wallet also lying on the floor, but a little distance away?'

'There was also the upturned vase', Corby said stiffly.

'Yes, I'm much obliged. I was trying to dissociate the disorder caused by a struggle with her assailant from other disorder. You follow me? The only sign of *other* disorder was the notecase lying, I think, somewhere over by the window?'

'Yes', Corby said, in a faintly grudging tone.

'Thank you, Captain Corby. That was all I wanted to ask you.'

Corby blinked uncertainly, as though half suspecting he was the victim of a practical joke. Why, there hadn't been a single question in cross-examination about the phone call his aunt had made to him on the morning of her death. The phone call about which the police had pretended to be so worried. He shot an accusing look at Steadman sitting at the table in the well of the court.

'Thank you, Captain Corby', the judge said, breaking in on his bemused thoughts.

'Ajit Singh', Mr. Freebody announced, rising to his feet, and adding helpfully to the judge, 'Page seven of the depositions, my lord.'

A bewildered-looking Ajit now came drifting into court transported in the wake of his interpreter.

As he reached the witness-box, Superintendent Blaker leaned across the table to Steadman and whispered in a tone of grim satisfaction, 'He won't try any more of that nonsense about not being clean.' With an effort Steadman roused himself from the torpor that was fast overtaking him.

'What form of oath does the witness wish to take?' Mr. Justice Gooch inquired agreeably.

'On this holy book, sair', the interpreter replied in a proprietorial tone, indicating a volume the size of an encyclopædia which the usher had balanced precariously on the ledge.

'Very well, let him be sworn.'

' 'Scuse, please, sair', the interpreter went on, oblivious of Blaker's sudden and furious stare. 'He would like first to wash his hands before touching the holy book.'

'Certainly', the judge said equably.

A small bowl of water was fetched and into this Ajit dipped his fingers without apparent enthusiasm, while people watched with all the fascination of a good conjurer's audience.

'Give him something to dry them with', Mr. Justice Gooch said. Superintendent Blaker's handkerchief seemed to be all that was available for this purpose and with considerable reluctance he proffered it. It was with an even greater grimace of distaste that he replaced it in his pocket.

When Mr. Cleaver rose to cross-examine, Ajit's evidence was to the staunch effect that Lucas was the person he had seen on the outskirts of Five Meadows on the morning of the murder.

'What made you come forward to the police and say you'd seen the accused?' Mr. Cleaver asked as his first question, and with an underlying note of aggression in his tone that had been missing when he cross-examined Miss Chatt and Captain Corby.

'I not quite understand', the interpreter said.

'You don't have to', Mr. Cleaver replied testily. 'Kindly interpret my question to the witness.'

The interpreter's eyes narrowed in an expression of dislike, but he turned to Ajit and spat out some angry-sounding words.

'The witness, Ajit, not understand either', he said, swinging back to Mr. Cleaver again.

'What prompted the witness to go to the police?' Mr. Justice Gooch broke in patiently. 'It's quite a simple question that counsel has asked.'

The interpreter gave the judge an attentive nod as though to indicate they understood each other, and said simply:

'I prompt him, sair.'

'You prompted him?' Mr. Cleaver echoed in a loud, scandalized voice across the tense courtroom. 'You mean you put him up to this?'

Mr. Justice Gooch smiled thinly. 'I'm not sure that you're entitled to question the interpreter, Mr. Cleaver. But I agree that we must clear up this matter.' Turning towards the witness-box and speaking with great judicial earnestness, he went on, 'Are you saying, Mr. Interpreter, that it was at your instigation that the witness came forward to the police?'

'Yes, sair.'

'And what were the circumstances of your doing so?'

'After he tell me that he see . . .'

Holding up a hand, the judge broke in quickly, 'Are you saying that as a result of something said to you by the witness, you advised him to make that known to the police?'

'Exactly so, sair.'

'I think that clears up the point, Mr. Cleaver.'

'Yes, m'lord. I'm much obliged, though I must say to your lordship that I think it's most unfortunate—and I deliberately use a neutral expression—that a friend of the witness should have been brought along as interpreter.' Out of the corner of his eye, he noticed two jurors nod and was about to embroider the theme further when Mr. Justice Gooch stopped him.

The clerk of the court turned round and spoke to the judge, who then looked down his nose at Mr. Freebody, who had been holding a frantically whispered conversation with Paul Steadman.

'Perhaps I can explain, m'lord', Mr. Freebody said with bland assurance. 'I understand that the witness speaks a very unusual dialect—a blend of two village dialects, in fact—and that this interpreter is the only person who has been found who can converse with him in his mother tongue. Efforts were made to secure the services of someone not acquainted with the witness but have been unsuccessful.'

'Ajit and I come from the same village, sair', the interpreter added politely.

Mr. Justice Gooch sighed. 'You'd better continue your cross-examination, Mr. Cleaver', he said, with a forbearing air.

Mr. Cleaver fixed the witness with a wintry look.

'I'm suggesting that you never saw Lucas that morning at all and that you're quite mistaken in saying that you did?'

'I see him', said the witness excitedly in halting English.

The interpreter frowned and barked out a staccato sentence. Then turning to the court, he explained, 'Ajit speak very little English. I tell him not to.'

After this further diversion, Mr. Cleaver pressed home his attack. He suggested that the witness was mistaken if not actually malicious and that he had reasons—those put forward by Mr. Macready in the lower court—for bearing personal animosity against Lucas.

For the most part, Ajit replied with monosyllables and indifferent shrugs, which came through the interpreter, however, as vehement denials, and a stubborn maintenance of his original testimony.

Eventually Ajit was allowed to leave the box, a thin, bewildered, unhappy-looking man from a distant Indian village whom one side put forward as a witness of simple truth and the other assailed as a mendacious schemer. As he took a seat and sat staring ahead of him with an utterly blank expression, Paul Steadman, who was watching him thoughtfully, fell to wondering what was going on in that narrow brown head.

His place in the witness-box was taken by Dr. Innes, whose second home it was. When Mr. Cleaver rose to cross-examine him, the two men exchanged the quick glittering smiles of contestants in the boxing ring.

'You've told us, Dr. Innes, that the cause of death in this case was suffocation?'

'That is so.'

'That the blow from the poker was not a contributory cause.'

'No, it had no direct bearing on her death.'

'I'm much obliged. Now supposing . . .'

'Mr. Cleaver', the judge's cool voice broke in. 'Forgive my interrupting you, but as I understand it, your defence is that your client had nothing at all to do with this crime; that he was elsewhere at the time of its commission.'

'That is so, m'lord.'

'How does it assist your case then to cross-examine Dr. Innes on details of his medical findings, if your client denies all responsibility for the infliction of the injuries?' Mr. Justice Gooch cocked his head at defending counsel and smiled inquiringly.

Mr. Cleaver listened with an air of rapt respect as the judge spoke, then he said, 'I'm most grateful to your lordship for raising this matter and if I may say so with great respect I do entirely concur in your lordship's view. . . .'

'I haven't expressed any view, Mr. Cleaver; merely asked you to clarify your defence for my assistance.'

'Quite so, m'lord, and I welcome the opportunity of doing so. My client's defence is, of course, that he didn't commit this crime, *but*, as your lordship will in due course be directing the jury, the onus of proving the charge is upon the Crown and in those circumstances I would submit that I am entitled, if the evidence justifies my doing so, to suggest to the jury that, apart from my client denying all knowledge of this crime, the Crown have in fact failed to prove that murder was committed.' Mr. Cleaver paused and a deathly silence hung over the court.

'And it is to that end that your cross-examination of this witness is directed?' Mr. Justice Gooch inquired.

'Precisely, m'lord.'

'Yes', Mr. Justice Gooch said, dubiously pursing his lips. 'Very well, Mr. Cleaver.'

'Dr. Innes, I needn't waste undue time on this, but the position is as follows, is it not: that the deceased might have rolled over on to this cushion after her assailant had departed?'

The witness fingered his lower lip and looked thoughtful.

'Most improbable, I should say.'

'But possible?'

'A very outside possibility.'

'Was there any blood-staining on the cushion?' the judge interjected.

'Yes, my lord, on its under side where it had been in contact with blood on the floor.'

'But none on the surface against which the deceased's head had lain?'

'No, my lord, since the only injury was on the *back* of the head and she lay, of course, face downwards.'

'Yes, thank you, doctor.' Mr. Justice Gooch motioned defending counsel to go on, but Mr. Cleaver, who had been having a whispered conversation with his junior, resumed his seat without further questions.

'I think it's better not to pursue that further', he said, leaning forward to speak to Mr. Macready. 'It's not an awfully good point unless one has the judge with one and I don't think we have.' Macready nodded sagely. 'We can have a much better go at Renshaw.'

Steadman, who had overheard this exchange, grinned across at Blaker, who merely raised an eyebrow.

It was about a quarter of an hour later that Mr. Cleaver, in fact, rose to cross-examine the Director of the laboratory.

'First let us deal with the footprint', he said, with an air of assured authority, holding up Dave Lucas's left shoe, which was alleged to have made the print. 'Do you agree, Dr. Renshaw, that this shoe is a cheap, mass-produced one?'

'I do.'

'Will you accept from me that it is a type which is manufactured by the thousand?'

'Certainly.'

'And consequently that there were probably thousands of men wearing that precise style of shoe on the day that Mrs. Easterberg met her death?'

'Ah! But not with all their soles worn to the same pattern.'

Mr. Cleaver gave a patient sigh and cast the jury a look which was intended to alienate any sympathies they might nurture towards the witness.

'Dr. Renshaw,' he said in a quietly chiding tone, 'I take it you're not suggesting that no two people can cause the same type of wear to a shoe?'

'No, I never . . . .'

'No, I didn't think you could mean anything so sweeping as that', Mr. Cleaver interjected smoothly. Dr. Renshaw glared.

'But that shoe you're holding in your hand, sir, shows wear to the sole identical with the pattern of the print I saw in the flower bed.'

'I'm sure it does if you tell us so. But'—and here Mr. Cleaver drew himself up like a king cobra about to strike—'you're not going to tell the jury that some other shoe couldn't have made that print?'

'How can I? I'm giving evidence of a scientific fact.'

'Exactly', Mr. Cleaver boomed. 'All you're saying is that in your *opinion* this shoe appears to have made that print, but that you can't exclude the possibility that it was made by a similar shoe.'

'I'm saying,' Dr. Renshaw said, in a dangerously quiet tone, 'that in my opinion that shoe made that print.'

'Very well', Mr. Cleaver remarked, as though he and the jury had been sufficiently wearied by the witness. 'Let me come now to the debris you found in the turn-ups of the accused's trousers. I gather the suggestion is that it came from the pampas grass in the upturned vase in the deceased lady's bedroom?'

'It is similar to that.'

'And similar to pampas grass anywhere?'

'Yes.'

'Is it within your knowledge that there is pampas grass growing along the banks of a stream which runs in the vicinity of Five Meadows Chase?'

'Yes.'

'You've seen it there yourself?'

'I have.'

'You can't say, can you, Dr. Renshaw, that what you found in the trouser turn-ups didn't in fact get there when the accused worked for Mrs. Easterberg and used to go walking by the stream?'

'That is possible. But it means that it had been there much longer than if it came from what was found in the bedroom.'

'*You* may brush out your trouser turn-ups regularly, Dr. Renshaw, but that doesn't mean that everyone does.'

The witness sniffed disdainfully and gave a shrug. It was easy for the lawyers to be clever, just as it was for a schoolteacher whose pupils couldn't answer back. Chin cupped in hand, Steadman watched him with twinkling amusement.

For the rest of the day witnesses came and went, but with no startling developments.

Jean, who was the first in the box after the lunch adjournment, looked piteously unhappy as Mr. Freebody coaxed her evidence from her. She had constantly to be exhorted to speak up and nobody could fail to observe the longing glances she cast at the man in the dock. He, however, seemed no more aware of her presence than he had been of the others. The trial might have been going on in a foreign tongue for all the attention he was paying to the proceedings.

Mr. Cleaver asked her but three questions in cross-examination and then, saying that he wished to spare her from further ordeal, sat down with another winning look at the jury.

It was shortly after twelve o'clock on the second day of the trial that Mr. Freebody announced, 'That is the case for the crown, my lord.'

'I'll call the prisoner', Mr. Cleaver immediately said.

Escorted by a prison officer, Lucas left the dock and made his way to the witness-box, where he took the oath and stared about him like someone just coming out of a long dream.

Mr. Cleaver's first question fell with quietly dramatic effect, so that even Paul Steadman found himself, absurdly, holding his breath.

'Did you murder Mrs. Easterberg, Lucas?'

'No, sir.'

'Where were you that day?'

'In London, sir.'

'Can you be more specific? What part of London?'

'In Bermondsey.'

'Doing what?'

'Just wandering around.'

'You were out of work still at that time?'

'Yes, sir.'

'Were you with anyone that day; anyone who can support your word?'

Lucas shook his head miserably. 'No, sir. One day was like another that week. I can't remember who I talked to on that particular one. I must have talked to someone, but . . . but . . . I haven't had a chance of finding out if they might remember.'

'Why did you move away up to north London after the murder?'

'Because I was frightened, sir, when I read in the papers that the police were looking for me.'

'Why were you frightened?'

'Because the papers made it sound as though they thought I'd killed Mrs. Easterberg.'

'Is that all?'

'I reckoned, sir, that it'd be best if I lay low until they'd found out who really'd done it.'

'Did you ever return to Five Meadows after you left Mrs. Easterberg's employ?'

'No, sir, I was in London all the time.'

'Do you know the witness Ajit Singh?'

'Yes, sir. I once told him to keep away from my girl and he threatened me.'

At this point there were confused cries from the back of the court, 'Not true, not true.'

'Silence', shouted the usher.

Mr. Cleaver went on, 'I want you to tell my lord and the jury how you got on with Mrs. Easterberg, Lucas.'

Lucas half-turned to face the twelve jurors whose heads were turned in his direction.

'She was good to me. She seemed to like me. She told me several times that my eyes were her favourite blue.'

'Did you nurse any grievance against her afterwards?'

'No.'

'I want you to tell the court what you were really doing up by her bedroom that day she found you there.'

Lucas nodded and passed his tongue over his lips.

'Well, you see, sir, one of my jobs was to clean the shoes which was always put out in the scullery for me. That morning I got called away before I'd finished 'em, but when I came back, I found they'd already been collected. I presumed it must be Mrs. Easterberg herself and that she hadn't noticed I'd not done the job proper so I thought I'd better go and get 'em from her room.'

'And it was when you were about to enter her bedroom that she found you?'

'Yes, sir, she suddenly came out of the bathroom.'

'Why didn't you tell her what you've just told my lord and the jury?'

'I tried to, but she wouldn't listen. She wouldn't listen to me at all, sir. She just shouted at me that I'd have to go.'

Mr. Cleaver turned a page of his brief. 'How often do you brush out the turn-ups of your trousers?'

Lucas grinned sheepishly. 'I never have, sir.'

'Did you ever go for walks in the fields and by the stream near Mrs. Easterberg's house?'

'Often, sir.'

'It has been said that when you were arrested you had over twenty pounds in your possession. Was that money you stole from Mrs. Easterberg?'

'No, sir.'

'Where did it come from?'

'I'd borrowed it from a friend.'

'His name?'

'Lennie Bernie, sir.'

'When had you borrowed it?'

'After I'd read about the police looking for me and had decided to lay up.'

Mr. Cleaver bent down to whisper to his junior and then said, 'That's all I have to ask the witness, my lord.'

There was an anticipatory rustle as Mr. Freebody stood up, for this was a moment of drama in every criminal trial. The cross-examination of the prisoner.

'You're an accomplished liar, aren't you, Lucas?'

'I've told the truth, sir.'

'We will see.'

For the next forty minutes Mr. Freebody drove home his questions with relentless tenacity and at the end Lucas looked tensely pale.

'He stood up to that hammering rather well', Mr. Cleaver whispered approvingly to Macready. He looked across at the jury who, however, were giving nothing away. And Mr. Cleaver and Mr. Freebody both knew better than to try and see a reflection of their own feelings about a case in a jury's expression.

As Lucas returned to his place in the yawning dock Steadman began idly doodling: his own few doubts still remained unresolved. Mr. Cleaver announced that his next and only other witness was Mr. Leonard Bernie.

Bernie was clearly ill at ease in the box and inherently suspicious of anything pertaining to the law. His evidence, however, was short and he confirmed that he had indeed lent the prisoner twenty pounds around the stated date.

Mr. Freebody seemed uncertain how to tackle this piece of evidence in cross-examination and finished by suggesting somewhat perfunctorily that if he ever had lent Lucas any money it had been on some entirely different occasion.

'Wrong', Lennie Bernie had said truculently, and Mr. Freebody had sat down as though the matter was not one worth bothering about.

The defence having called evidence in addition to that of the prisoner, it fell to Mr. Cleaver to make the first closing speech to the jury.

'Members of the jury,' he began with slow solemnity, giving each word its fullest weight, 'in a short while you will be retiring to consider your verdict, to decide whether this young man, David Lucas, shall step forth into the streets outside a free man or whether he shall leave this august building huddled in the back of a grim prison van.' His voice sank an octave. 'Members of the jury, it is that which you will shortly have to decide.

'Before I ask you to consider with me the evidence on which the prosecution are inviting you to convict this young man of capital murder, let me remind you—as indeed his lordship shortly will—that you have to be satisfied on the evidence of the prosecution that murder has in fact been committed. Are you, members of the jury?' Here Mr. Cleaver cast a quick, questioning look at Mr. Justice Gooch. But the judge was turning the pages of his notebook and did not respond. 'Are you satisfied that this was murder? We know after all that the blow with the poker had nothing to do with this unfortunate woman's death. But how do we know that she wasn't instrumental in causing her own death: that it was not she herself who placed the cushion on the floor beneath her head? It's a possibility, isn't it, members of the jury? And it follows, of course, that if that is what did happen, then she was not murdered.' This time Mr. Cleaver felt the judge's eye turned on him and he went on hastily. 'But let us now look at the evidence on which this charge rests, and let us consider it against the wholehearted denials of complicity in this terrible crime which the accused has made from the very beginning. First let us consider what I may term the direct evidence. What is it? The evidence of that wretched Indian who says he saw the prisoner in Five Meadows on the morning of the crime. I call him wretched, members of the jury, because wasn't that just the way he looked? Dragged to court by that other Indian gentleman who acted as interpreter, and, you may think, was a good deal more than that. I am sure you will not be surprised at my asking you—and asking you with complete confidence—to disregard utterly the evidence of such a witness. If Lucas was in Five Meadows that day, isn't it truly remarkable that no one else saw him? Perhaps one or two of you—and alas it is not given to me to look inside your heads and see how best I can help you—are wondering why that witness should have given that evidence if, as I strongly suggest, it be not true.' Mr. Cleaver rocked himself back on his heels and scanned the jury's faces. 'You will remember from my cross-examination of P.C. Green that he told you one of the first things Ajit Singh did when he came to the police station was to claim a reward. Isn't that the whole clue to his evidence? That, coupled with the fact of his malice towards Lucas because Lucas had once had occasion to tell him to keep away from his girl-friend.' Mr. Cleaver paused, then said with an air of well-assumed confidence, 'I don't want to labour a point which I'm quite certain you have well in mind, so I'll leave it there.

'Now, coming to the indirect evidence. What does that amount to? It amounts, in the main, to two matters. One the shoe-print; the other the debris found in the trouser turn-ups. Those, as I understand their case, are two pieces of evidence on which the prosecution place great reliance. What reliance do you place, members of the jury, on a shoe-print which could have been made by literally a thousand different shoes, and on particles of pampas grass which could have got into the prisoner's trouser turn-ups on any one of many occasions when he was working at Mrs. Easterberg's?'

Mr. Cleaver proceeded to belittle the scientific evidence with considerable eloquence and then went on to pour gentle scorn on other points which Mr. Freebody had stressed in his opening speech: Lucas's knowledge of the habits of Mrs. Easterberg's household, his disappearance immediately after the crime and his possession of a considerable sum of cash when he was arrested.

At last he had completed his dissection of the evidence against his client and launched into his peroration.

'And what is left, members of the jury? Denials, stout denials by Lucas that he was anywhere near Five Meadows when this crime was committed. Are you, in the face of those denials, repeated on oath before you in this court, going to convict him on the evidence of a witness whose prime aim in coming forward was to claim a reward! On the flimsiest scientific evidence that a jury can ever have been invited to consider! Members of the jury, you will not, I know, allow yourselves to transmute suspicion into evidence for the sake of finding Lucas a convenient scapegoat. You will have regard only for *evidence* itself and if you do that then I say one verdict and one verdict only is open to you. Namely, to find the prisoner not guilty of this charge.'

Mr. Freebody rose to his feet with the indulgent air of one confident that he can soon put things back in their proper perspective.

'What an unfortunate child of circumstance the prisoner has been, has he not, members of the jury? How outrageously fortune has treated him! That is, if you accept all that my learned friend has just said to you. Do you really think it is pure coincidence that Ajit Singh saw Lucas shortly before the crime; shortly before someone—and who else but Lucas—wearing that shoe, exhibit fourteen, made a print in the flower-bed as he fled from the scene of the crime. Coincidence, members of the jury, or a natural sequence of events involving a person who is not only identified by an eye-witness but, in addition, by the distinguishing feature of his shoes.

'I venture to suggest to you that the case for the Crown remains unchallenged in its vital aspects; that the evidence is unshaken on all the major issues.'

Mr. Freebody went on to expand this argument and to demolish with forensic relish those put forward by Mr. Cleaver.

'Members of the jury, it is not for the Crown to press for a conviction in this or any other case. The Crown's duty is to lay the facts before you and to invite you to draw what they believe to be the proper inferences. In this present case, members of the jury, there is, I suggest, one overwhelming and inescapable inference: namely that the prisoner committed this crime. And if that is the view which you take when you have sifted and considered all the evidence, then it will be your duty, in accordance with the oaths which you have taken, to find this young man guilty of murder, murder committed moreover in the course or furtherance of theft.'

All eyes now switched to Mr. Justice Gooch, who half-turned so that he faced the jury and removed his spectacles with a commanding gesture.

'Members of the jury, the accused young man, David Lucas, stands charged with murder committed, it is said, in the course or furtherance of theft, and, as in every criminal case, the burden of proving the charge to your satisfaction rests upon the prosecution. Now what, here, has to be proved? First, that Mrs. Easterberg was murdered; and murder, members of the jury, is the unlawful killing of another person either with intent so to kill or at least with intent to do grievous bodily harm. If you are satisfied that Mrs. Easterberg was deliberately struck with this poker and that as a result she fell face forward into the cushion on the floor and was so suffocated, or that having fallen on to the floor the person who had struck her placed the cushion beneath her head for some reason of his own—to try, perhaps, to ameliorate the damage he had already caused—then that in law would amount to murder.

'Mr. Cleaver suggested to you that the deceased may herself have brought the cushion on to the floor after her assailant had fled, but there is no evidence of that: indeed it is a suggestion which flies in the face of the medical evidence. And you, as both counsel have been at pains to remind you,' Mr. Justice Gooch went on dryly, 'are concerned only with evidence which has been given in this court.'

From this he went on to review the evidence and to comment on various aspects of it, though carefully main-saining an impartial balance. It was indeed a scrupulously fair summing-up; so fair that Mr. Cleaver realized that if the verdict went against Lucas, there would be little or nothing on which to base an appeal.

Mr. Freebody, who also recognized its fairness, was satisfied, since he reckoned the prosecution would triumph on an impartial tally of points.

About Ajit Singh the judge was particularly careful not to express a personal opinion. He stressed the great importance of his evidence, said the jury would no doubt weigh with care the criticisms which had been levelled against him and commented that it was entirely a matter for them, having seen and heard the witness in the box, to decide what credence to accord his testimony.

When it came to the scientific evidence, Mr. Justice Gooch was equally fair, but in stressing the high importance of the shoe-print evidence it was possible to detect his own acceptance of it. Mr. Cleaver looked anxiously at the jury to see which way they appeared to be leaning, but all he observed were twelve stolidly intent expressions as they listened to his lordship like a group of sinners who realized this was their last chance of snatching salvation.

The summing-up had lasted seventy-five minutes and it was a quarter to four as the judge concluded, 'That is all the assistance I think I can give you, members of the jury, and I now ask you to retire and consider your verdict, which, as I've explained, can be one of three. Guilty of capital murder, guilty of ordinary murder if you are satisfied that it was the accused who murdered Mrs. Easterberg but do not find it proved to your satisfaction that it was done in the course or furtherance of theft; and lastly, not guilty.'

He now leaned back in his chair and surveyed their anxious faces as the jury bailiff swore to 'keep this jury in some convenient private place and to suffer no one to speak to them, unless it be to ask them if they are agreed upon their verdict'. As Mr. Justice Gooch watched them, he reflected that it was invariably his lay friends who decried the jury system. The legal profession was aware of its value and in no case was it more valuable than in one such as this where the application of commonsense to the facts should produce the right answer, which was . . . Mr. Justice Gooch felt reasonably certain that Lucas was guilty but he was not at all sure how he would vote if he were himself on the jury. The thought was still in his mind as he retired to his room.

'Guilty or not guilty', he said to his clerk with a smile as he sipped a cup of tea.

His clerk looked up in surprise.

'Of course he did it, sir.'

'I think so too, but will the jury?'

Outside the courtroom Paul Steadman and James Macready were standing together.

Macready was fidgety. He had put a tremendous lot of work into the case and its outcome meant much more to him than it did to Steadman, who had handled almost a hundred murder cases since he had been on the staff of the Director of Public Prosecutions and who had seldom felt any emotion about any of them, beyond an occasional melancholy at man's inherited plight.

'How long do you think they'll be?' Macready asked abruptly.

Steadman smiled. 'My dear chap, juries are quite unpredictable. You know that!'

It was, in fact, two hours and ten minutes before word went round that they were ready.

The courtroom filled and an expectant hush fell as the clerk of the court did a roll call of the jurors' names. Everyone scanned their expressions, but they looked remarkably the same as they had two hours and ten minutes before.

Those who held that you could always know a jury's verdict by whether or not they looked at the prisoner on his return to the dock were disconcerted to observe that some of them did and others ostentatiously did not. A disagreement!

Mr. Justice Gooch took his seat and everyone followed suit save Lucas, who stood staring with fixed intensity at the royal coat of arms behind the judge's seat.

The clerk of the court rose.

'Members of the jury, are you agreed upon your verdict?'

The foreman stood up.

'We are, my lord.'

'Do you find the prisoner David Lucas guilty or not guilty of murder committed in the course or furtherance of theft?'

'Not guilty.'

A gasp, followed by a rustle of excitement, rippled through the court.

'Do you find him guilty or not guilty of murder?'

'Not guilty.'

'Let the prisoner be discharged', Mr. Justice Gooch announced, in cold, judicial tones.

The trial of David Lucas was over.

THIRTEEN

Miss Chatt threaded her way through the crowd outside the courtroom. She had caught sight of Captain Corby and felt this was an opportunity to say good-bye to him. It seemed unlikely that she would be seeing him again.

'I just wanted to say good-bye, Captain Corby', she said a trifle breathlessly as she reached his side.

He gave her a preoccupied nod. 'That was a scandalous triumph of injustice.' Miss Chatt made sympathetic sounds. This was not the moment to indicate that she herself was secretly pleased with the verdict. 'A young murderer at large and the police powerless to do anything about it', Corby went on in the same bitter tone. 'Small wonder that decent citizens are sometimes provoked into taking the law into their own hands.'

Miss Chatt nodded earnestly. 'Will the police do anything more?'

'What more can they do? They know as well as anyone else that Lucas is guilty, but a half-witted jury having acquitted him, that's an end of the matter. If he's got sufficient impudence he can even confess the crime now and nobody can do a damned thing.'

They had reached the bottom of the stairs and were moving towards the main entrance to the building.

'Well, Captain Corby, perhaps this is where I ought to say good-bye', Miss Chatt said, starting to remove her glove. They shook hands.

'Good-bye, Miss Chatt. Thanks for all you did for my aunt. I'll be glad to give you a reference if you need one in getting a new job.'

'That's most kind of you, Captain Corby. I propose to take a little rest for a few weeks, staying with my cousin who lives in Harrow.' She was about to move away but something in his expression caused her to hesitate.

Speaking with obvious embarrassment he said, 'I should have liked to have been able to show my appreciation of your services in more substantial form, but, as you know, my aunt's will . . .'

Blushing hard, Miss Chatt broke in hastily, 'I'm sure I'm most grateful to you for so much as thinking of such a thing. I quite understand the position, so please don't feel badly about it.'

They shook hands again and parted before either needed to be further embarrassed.

By the time that Steadman and Macready had collected up their papers, the courtroom was deserted.

'Well, did he or didn't he?' Macready asked, with a sidelong glance at Steadman, as he fastened the catch of his briefcase.

There was a thoughtful pause, then Steadman replied with a short, good-natured laugh, 'He did.'

'But you hesitated.'

'Ye-es, but I still think he did it.'

Macready cast a quick look round the court. 'So, as a matter of fact, do I. Though, mark you, I also think that the jury were right to acquit. They were left with too many doubts.'

Paul Steadman pursed his lips. There had always been features of the case which had puzzled him and he wondered whether Macready knew anything which had not come out in court. Almost in answer to his thoughts, Macready remarked suddenly, 'You know, he never told me a single thing beyond what he'd said to the police when they arrested him. He's stuck to his denials right through.'

Steadman tucked a pile of papers beneath his arm and prepared to go. 'He's obviously a young man with an exceptionally strong nerve. Wonder if we shall ever know the truth.'

In the public house across the road, Manton, Yates, Blaker and two of his officers were standing in various attitudes of morose contemplation.

'Pah! Twelve good men and true, indeed!' Blaker remarked explosively, draining his glass and passing it across the counter for a refill. 'It makes you wild, all the bloody time and energy you put into this job, just for twelve morons to cock a snook at you—and at justice and the rest of the community.'

'Nothing you can do about it', Manton said, a trifle edgily.

'Huh! And all the pious hot air that's spouted about our precious jury system! It makes me sick every time I listen to it.'

'Still nothing you can do about it!'

'I'm not so sure', Blaker said savagely.

'What then?'

'Make public the names of jurors who've acquitted guilty men so that next time the people they've let out want to go robbing or housebreaking they know where the dolts live.'

Manton gave an unamused laugh. He was in no mood for Blaker's wild verbal swipes at society.

'Hello there, gentlemen. Trying to drown your

sorrows?' It was one of the crime reporters who had come up and who spoke. 'Suppose you've no doubt he did do it?'

'No more than anyone has who's in their right senses', Blaker snarled.

'So there's no question of your reopening inquiries?'

Manton shook his head.

'Not unless you put us on to something', he said dryly.

The newspaper man laughed.

' 'Fraid not. I don't know a thing. Which is a pity because it's a case with a nicely fermenting background. All the business about the old girl's will and that garage chap, I mean.'

'Did you catch Lucas when he left court?' Manton asked with interest.

'No, I wasn't bothering to try and see him. I had a word with his girl-friend, though. She was waiting for him. I asked her what her plans were. Were they going away to get married or what? But just then one of your side-kicks came up and piloted her away.' Manton grinned. 'But I had a cosy little chat with one of the jurors.' He paused, gratified by the reaction this piece of news brought.

'Well, what'd he say?' Blaker barked while Manton took a step closer.

The reporter grinned mischievously. 'Oh, he said that none of them really doubted Lucas had done it, but they didn't feel they could be quite certain enough, having regard to the fact that his life was in their hands.'

'But it wasn't, and the judge went out of his way to tell them that the penalty was no concern of theirs', Blaker said angrily.

'But you know what juries are, Super! Also I gathered they took rather a fancy to Lucas.'

'Sentimentalists! Have a baby face and you can commit murder with impunity, I suppose.'

The reporter was enjoying himself. 'The fellow I spoke to—he was two from the left in the front row—felt you'd done the best you could but that your evidence fell just a bit short.'

'Another double Scotch!' Blaker demanded, sliding his glass across the counter.

'I don't know!' Manton observed with a sigh. 'Seems to me a complete waste of time judges explaining all about reasonable doubt and the degree of proof required and the rest of it. In the end a jury throws everything into the pot—bits of evidence, hunks of prejudice, slices of sentiment, preconceived ideas, red herrings, theories about capital punishment and the wicked ways of the police. They then give it a good stir and see which bits come floating to the top.' He paused, took a gulp at his beer and added, 'One thing that's quite certain is that it's always the evidence which sinks to the bottom.'

The Old Bailey stood dark and silent when they emerged. Manton's gaze went up to the figure of Justice that crowned the great dome of the building.

'You want your scales seeing to, my woman', he murmured in a reproachful tone.

FOURTEEN

MANTON was sitting in his office at the Yard the next morning, tackling arrears of paper work and wondering whether he was likely to come in for any criticism for his handling of the Lucas case (there was always a tendency to judge police officers by results), when the phone suddenly rang.

'Manton here', he announced laconically.

'It's Lucas, sir.'

'Yes, what do you want, Lucas?' he asked, with a mixture of weariness and hostility.

'I want to see you, sir.'

'What about?'

'About the case. There's . . . there's something I'd like to tell you.'

'Go ahead then.'

'I can't sort of explain it over the phone.'

'Why not?' Manton's tone was unsympathetic.

'It's kind of a long story, sir. Not the sort to tell on the phone.'

'Look, Lucas, the jury acquitted you and the case is over and I'm in no mood to be fooled with.' There was a silence from the other end of the line and Manton felt a faint pang. Whatever his personal feelings, he had no official right to head Lucas off without first knowing what it was about. 'Well, I'll be here all the afternoon, you can come and see me if you want. Where are you speaking from, by the way?'

'A public call box. I'd sooner not come to your place. Can't we meet in a café?'

Manton's wariness bristled like a frightened hedgehog.

'Is this some lark a newspaper's put you up to, Lucas? Because if it is . . .'

'No, I swear it isn't. I've got something really important to tell you, sir; something you'll be grateful to me for.' He added in a disarming tone, 'You can't blame me for not wanting to come to your place, sir. I don't feel at home there. It'll be different on neutral ground.'

Manton looked at his watch and thought rapidly.

'All right, Lucas, I'll meet you at half-past three this afternoon at . . .' And he proceeded to give directions to a small café in one of the side streets off the Strand. 'But I warn you if this is some trick or stunt, you'll regret you ever made this phone call.'

After he had rung off, Manton sat for some time in contemplation of the opposite wall. If Lucas was playing the fool it would be just too bad for him. If, on the other hand he *had* got some fresh piece of information to impart, it would be likely to involve further, and probably fruitless, work for himself. Lightly-made complaints and frivolous allegations by the public frequently took up days of an officer's time.

At a quarter-past three he collected Sergeant Yates from the room which he shared with three other detective sergeants and the two men left the building together. They walked along the embankment as far as Charing Cross bridge and then turned up towards the Strand. Big Ben had just struck the half hour when Manton pushed open the door of the café and stepped inside.

Lucas, who was sitting alone at a table at the far end, looked up as he heard the doorbell ping. Manton glanced round, winking a greeting at the aproned owner whom he had known since his early days as a young constable stationed at Bow Street, and satisfied himself that there were no lurking newspaper reporters.

Pulling up a chair to Lucas's table he sat down, followed by Sergeant Yates.

No one spoke, but under Manton's steady stare, Lucas began to fidget uneasily.

'Well?' Manton said at last.

Lucas spooned some tea out of the cup in front of him and drank it.

'Goin' to have a cupper tea, sir?'

'On you? Sure.' Almost before he had spoken the owner came from behind the steaming urns carrying two cups, which he placed before Manton and Yates.

'I imagine you still think I murdered the old girl, don't you?' Lucas asked, lighting a cigarette and noisily exhaling.

Manton's tone was dangerously quiet. 'Look, I've warned you, I'm in no mood for . . .'

'Well, the point is I never did', Lucas broke in. 'It wasn't me that killed her.'

'He must think, sir, that we want to hear those fairy stories he told the jury all over again.' Yates's tone was heavily sarcastic.

Manton's eyes narrowed. 'All right, you got away with it this time, Lucas, but don't let it make you think you can start crowing over us with impunity.'

'I'm trying to tell you, if you'll listen, that I didn't kill her but that I was there.'

In a second he had their rapt attention. Their heads bent over the table like a trio of conspirators.

'Meaning exactly what?'

'I hit her on the head with the poker all right. But that had nothing to do with her death, did it? The doctor said it didn't. He said how she suffocated with her face in that cushion, didn't he?' Lucas paused, his eyes urgently searching Manton's face. 'There wasn't any cushion on the floor when I left her, sir.'

FIFTEEN

MANTON stared at Lucas with unseeing eyes, his thoughts flying back over the events of recent weeks. He felt like a racing driver who completes a hazardous course only to be told that he was in fact disqualified soon after crossing the starting line.

He refocused his gaze.

'Go on,' he said flatly.

'Once a jury says you're not guilty, you can't be done again, can you?' Lucas asked, in a suddenly anxious tone. Manton nodded. It was near enough the truth. Lucas took a deep breath. 'Well, it was like you believed. I was sore at the old girl flinging me out and I thought I'd pay her back. I knew how she kept her money in various purses and that it'd be quite easy to get a few pickings. I thought Wednesday'd be a good day to go because Miss Chatt would be out and I knew Mrs. Winter and Mrs. Scarlon would still be away. I hitched a lift up the main road early that morning and then walked cross-country-like to her house.'

'Being seen by Ajit Singh.'

Lucas smirked. 'It was a bit of bad luck running into that little brown weasel. Anyway I got up to the house. There wasn't anyone about and I crept upstairs quiet-like and got into her bedroom.'

'And started to go through her drawers?'

'Didn't even have time to', Lucas said indignantly. 'Suddenly the door opened and the old girl herself came in.' He paused and shook his head reflectively. 'What an old battleaxe! She didn't yell out or anything, just picked up the poker and came for me. I was scared out of my pants. I couldn't get out of the room and all I could do was try and seize the poker from her. We had a helluva struggle—that was when that vase of fluffy stuff was knocked over. Eventually I got hold of the poker and I gave her a tap on the nut to quieten her down.' He stubbed out his cigarette and wiped his fingers along the edge of the table. 'I admit I hit her harder than I meant and she fell on to the floor. But there wasn't no cushion anywhere near her head, and I certainly didn't stop to make her comfy.'

'Which way did she fall?' Manton asked thoughtfully.

'On to her back.'

'And it was after that you went through the drawers and threw the wallet out on the floor?' Yates put in.

'Like hell, I didn't. I just legged it out of the window as fast as I could. Bloody nearly sprained my ankle in that flower-bed, too.'

'How'd the empty wallet get on the floor then?' Yates pressed.

'Same person as put the cushion under her head and turned her face down, I suppose.'

'Why did you leave by the window instead of by the door and stairs?'

'Haven't you guessed? 'Cause I heard someone coming along the landing, of course.'

Manton knew that it would save him endless trouble if he could discount everything that Lucas had said. But this was impossible, for he realized it was the truth. It fitted too well to be otherwise.

The hasty flight through the window which had puzzled Paul Steadman was now explained. Also why there had been blood on the floor but not on the surface of the cushion in which the old lady's head had lain. It was now starkly plain that someone had come into the room even as Lucas was scarcely out of it! Someone who had found Mrs. Easterberg lying unconscious on her back and who had rolled her over and placed a soft, suffocating cushion beneath her face. Someone, moreover, who had immediately sized up the situation and had added a touch by dropping the empty wallet on the floor. Something to put the police on to the trail of a burglar.

The implications made Manton's blood run chill, but he looked at Lucas with anything but kindliness.

'Why didn't you tell us this before?' he asked, though knowing what the answer would be.

' 'Cause you'd never have believed me and I'd have really been putting the rope round my neck. Also how'd I know she didn't die from the crack I gave her with the poker! It wasn't till I heard the doctor at the first court that I knew anything about her suffocating and about there being a pillow under her head. You never told me that!'

As Manton had known, it was the story of a criminal who, having denied all participation in a crime, is tied to that defence. Having said he wasn't present when the crime was committed, he couldn't turn round and say 'but it didn't happen that way'. All this was now very clear to Manton as he chewed savagely on his thoughts.

He looked balefully across the table at Lucas.

'And supposing the jury had convicted you, my friend, what were you going to do then?'

'I'd have told you the same thing, sir. I was going to tell Mr. Macready too.'

Manton's tone was solemn when he spoke. 'I think it's as well for you that the jury didn't find you guilty.'

Lucas swallowed hard and tried to grin.

At the sound of the door opening, the three of them looked up. Advancing towards their table was the crime reporter of the previous evening. A sharp look at Lucas told Manton that he didn't know the man.

'Well, well', the reporter said, with jovial suggestiveness. 'Mind if I join you?'

'We're just going', Manton replied, pushing back his chair and doing up a button of his jacket. 'All three of us', he added firmly.

'Pity! I'll just have to guess at the bits I don't know.' He looked from Manton to Yates with the smile of a spider deprived of its fly.

'Look, there's nothing. . . . Oh go to hell!' Manton turned away from the table. 'Come on, Dave.' Outside the café, he went on, 'You're coming back to the Yard with us where we're going to get this all down in writing, and you're going to sign it.'

'Who was that man?' Lucas asked, ignoring what Manton had just said.

'A newspaper fellow. Blast him! It's particularly important that the papers don't start any hares about this.'

'Huh?'

'If you didn't murder Mrs. Easterberg, someone else did. Someone who at the moment is well lulled into a false sense of security.' Manton's voice took on a note of quiet menace. 'Which is the way I want him to remain.'

SIXTEEN

To say that Lucas's statement caused consternation was to express matters mildly.

Superintendent Blaker came hurrying down to London and there was an immediate conference at the Director of Public Prosecutions' department, at which eight men sat round a large table and metaphorically chewed their nails. Eventually the Director himself asked:

'Who've we really got as suspects? By that, I mean people against whom there's a motive of some sort. I suppose there's the nephew. Who else?'

'Pringle, I'd say, sir', Manton added. 'They're the two most likely. In fact I don't think anyone else really comes into the picture.'

'Lewis Spicer?' Steadman suggested.

Manton made a dubious face. 'Not as likely as the other two, in my opinion, sir.'

'It's a question of cracking alibis', the Director observed.

'We've never taken a statement from Pringle about his movements that morning. We had no real cause to. By the time we knew he had a motive, we were looking for Lucas. If we go and see him now . . .' He made a gesture indicating the probable futility of such a move. 'Quite frankly, sir, if Pringle did it, I doubt whether we'll ever get evidence against him. He's a tough nut.'

The Director spoke again. 'He and Corby are the two most likely people to have gone to the house that morning. Each of them, I gather, used to pay regular visits and each of them was, so to speak, *persona grata*. By that, I mean they walked in and out without ringing front-door bells and the like.'

'That's so, sir', Manton agreed.

'And it also happens that they're the two with the most compelling motives.' He looked round the intent faces before going on, 'It may be a coincidence that one of them has both motive *and* opportunity; surely it's more than coincidence that both have.'

'We haven't mentioned the companion, Miss Chatt', Blaker suddenly said, in the silence that followed.

'Does anyone suggest she might have done it?' the Director asked with faint surprise. 'I thought she'd left the house and that you'd checked her movements.' He turned over the pages of the file before him. 'I see she says she drove up to London and visited the hairdresser.'

'We checked that she did that all right', Manton said. 'And as far as we know she had no motive.'

'Thought I better mention her all the same', Blaker remarked gruffly.

'No, on what you tell me,' the Director went on, 'I think Pringle and Corby are the two we'd better put under the microscope.'

Paul Steadman nodded. 'I believe more and more that a clue lies in that phone call the deceased made to Corby only an hour or so before she was murdered. Although she told him not to come up to the house until the afternoon, I think he knows more about it than he's told us and I wouldn't be surprised if he didn't in fact dash up there almost immediately. I'm sure the solution's all bound up with that and with the will and Pringle.'

'An interesting field for speculation', the Director broke in dryly. And on this note, the conference ended.

Back at the Yard, Manton, Blaker and Sergeant Yates went into further conclave.

'We'll re-check every detail in Corby's and Miss Chatt's statements', Manton said.

'I thought it was agreed, sir, that Corby and Pringle were our most likely suspects', Yates remarked.

'They are, but we're going to check on everyone who might have committed the crime, likely or unlikely.'

Blaker spoke. 'What I'd like to know is how we start checking on Pringle, and Spicer too for that matter, when we haven't even got a statement from either of them.'

'I've been thinking about that', Manton said thoughtfully. 'What about the postman, Sam Shoe?'

'What about him?'

'He delivers for the whole village. That means he must have called at Pringle's and Spicer's houses that morning within a short time of his calling at the Chase. We'll ask him if he remembers seeing either of them when he left their letters.'

'There mayn't have been any for them that particular morning', Blaker objected.

'It's more likely that there were. One's a writer, and they usually have a fair amount of correspondence. The other runs a garage and I shouldn't have thought that there were many days he didn't receive mail.'

Blaker pursed his lips, obviously unmoved by this argument. 'A postman doesn't necessarily see the people at whose houses he delivers letters.'

'Agreed', Manton said, with a faint note of exasperation in his voice. 'We may learn nothing, but at least it's worth trying.' He turned to Yates. 'Put through a call and find out where we can find Sam Shoe.'

'Here, I'd better do that through my headquarters', Blaker said, taking the telephone receiver from him.

It was to learn, however, that Shoe was off duty and not at home and that he was unlikely to return before bedtime.

'We'll get hold of him first thing in the morning', Manton said. 'Meanwhile I'm going through our file again.'

'Where do you think that'll get you?' Blaker asked.

'I don't know, but it's better than doing nothing and I can't think of anything more useful at the moment.'

Blaker looked about the room with a disgruntled air.

'If it wasn't Lucas who murdered the old girl, then it was either Corby or Pringle, but we're never going to be able to prove anything.'

'Maybe we shan't solve it, but there's a hell of a lot more inquiries to be made before we can properly report failure.'

'Well, I'm going to get back', Blaker remarked ill-humouredly. 'I'll expect you along first thing in the morning, is that it?"

'Yes; to see Sam Shoe. Perhaps you can arrange with the post office people to have him available.'

'All right, but I still don't think it'll get us anywhere.'

He went out, leaving Manton and Yates to exchange glances of relief. Manton said, 'If Blaker's right, then we'll have to tackle every person who might have been expected to have seen Corby about the time of the crime and find out if anyone did see him. Ditto with Pringle.' He sighed. 'The thing that bothers me is what's going to happen when all this further inquiry business bursts forth in the press.'

'It could flush out something to put us on the trail, sir.'

'It's much more likely to make the murderer redouble his guard.'

SEVENTEEN

'LOOK at this, Richard', Linda Corby said in a portentous tone, as she thrust the *Morning Echo* under her husband's nose at the same time as she placed a plate of scrambled eggs in front of him.

It was not the paper they regularly took and he asked sharply, 'Where'd this come from?'

'Mrs. Dove'—this was their daily woman—'she brought it. But read it.'

' "Rich Widow's killer still at large",' Corby read the headlines aloud. ' "Startling revelations by acquitted man start police on fresh inquiries. Dramatic developments expected following police conference with the Director of Public Prosecutions".' Frowning heavily, Corby looked up at his wife who still stood beside him, her mouth indignantly twitching. 'But . . . but this is . . . it's unheard of reopening a case after the jury's verdict. What's Lucas been up to?'

'It's the headlines I take exception to', Linda Corby said coldly. 'What do they mean by "killer still at large"?'

'They can't mean Lucas . . .'

'Of course it doesn't refer to Lucas.'

Their eyes met again, each searching the other's face for some comforting answer and finding none.

'But if Lucas didn't murder Aunt Sophie, who did?' Corby asked, with a set expression.

His wife nervously tapped her foot. 'Look, Richard, the police will almost certainly be back here checking on every little detail again, asking endless questions and generally making themselves unpleasant; that's what we've got to expect.'

'But I can't tell them any more than I have already. They can't possibly think that *I* had anything to do with Aunt Sophie's death.'

'What you don't know is what lies Lucas mayn't have told them. That's the point!' Linda Corby's tone was waspish. 'Anyway, I think it's absolutely disgraceful printing this sort of thing on the front page of the paper.'

'It'd be pretty bad on any page.'

'You know quite well what I mean. I think you should consult your solicitor to see what action can be taken to prevent such monstrous things being written.'

It was a pensive and shaken Corby who rose from the breakfast table and wandered off towards his greenhouses in the field at the back. He had nothing to fear, of course, but a resurgence of all the inevitable publicity was an utterly distasteful prospect.

Further along the village street, Lewis Spicer was reading the same newspaper report over his cup of breakfast chocolate. His expression was one of absorbed interest without trace of any personal anxiety.

This was splendid! Not only had the nice plump David Lucas got off, but he'd managed to turn the tables on his accusers. And who were his accusers? Spicer hadn't the slightest doubt that they were Captain Corby, aided and abetted by his wife. He had shown a superior contempt for Corby since they had first met soon after his, Spicer's, arrival in Five Meadows. Corby represented almost all that Spicer was wont to ridicule. He clung to tradition for tradition's sake and upheld, albeit ineffectively, the alleged virtues of his breed. How delicious to think that he might be unmasked as a murderer—as his aunt's murderer at that!

Spicer sipped abstractedly at his chocolate while his eyes remained glued to the newspaper.

When he had finished and had washed up the cup, he went upstairs to put on a pair of shoes.

This was no morning for work. He must be out and about the village, exchanging gossip and observing developments. It seemed that Mrs. Easterberg might bring him yet further copy. His expression was one of pleasurable anticipation as he closed the front door behind him and stepped out into the morning sunshine.

Farther still along the street, Bob Pringle gave some terse instructions to his mechanic and then went and shut himself in his tiny office. There, he pulled a well-folded newspaper from his jacket pocket and with expressionless eyes read through the report once more.

When he had finished he looked out of the window, scanning the forecourt of his premises. He half-expected to see a police-car drive up. But no one came, not even P.C. Green on his bicycle.

Well, to be forewarned was to be forearmed. He had withstood the gossip which had circulated when the contents of the old girl's will had become known, now he would withstand the fresh tide which the further police inquiries would undoubtedly provoke.

'Look, Violet, here's a piece all about your case.'

The speaker was Miss Chatt's cousin and the observation made as the two ladies sat facing each other at breakfast over boiled eggs. 'It says that Mrs. Easterberg's murderer is still at large and that dramatic disclosures have been made to the police by the man who was acquitted. It also says that the police are now closely re-examining the statements in their original dossier.' She looked over the top of the paper. 'Do tell me, dear, what do you think it's all about?'

'I've no idea', Miss Chatt replied faintly. 'No idea at all.'

'It says the police are making new inquiries in the Five Meadows district. You must be awfully glad you've left there, dear.'

'I am.'

'Though I suppose they might come and see you here.'

'I hope not.' Miss Chatt gave a little shiver. 'I thought it was going to be all over with Lucas's acquittal.'

'But it's as a result of something he's now told the police that their inquiries have started up again. At least that's what it says in the paper. What do you think it can be?'

Miss Chatt shook her head, more in dismissal of the subject than as a gesture of ignorance.

'Ah, well, I'll clear these things away, dear', her cousin said, rising briskly to her feet and stacking plates, cups and saucers on to a tray. She left the room with them. Miss Chatt waited till she heard washing-up in progress before stretching out a hand for the newspaper and quickly but intently reading through the report for herself, at the same time keeping a wary ear open for returning footsteps.

Paul Steadman drained his cup of coffee and pushed back his chair. Then, glancing at his watch, he got up.

'I must be off, sweetheart', he said. 'Now don't forget what I said, if Linda Corby rings up you must be very careful what you say to her.'

'Of course, darling.' His wife held a piece of toast vaguely in mid-air, as with a pencil in the other hand she scribbled in a notebook at her side.

'Don't let her start pumping you about the case.'

'No-o.'

'She'll probably try to find out whether her husband is under suspicion.'

'But he is, isn't he? You told me so last night', Jane Steadman said, suddenly looking up with a thoughtful expression. 'Poor old Linda! Her aunt murdered and her husband suspected of doing it!'

'Jane!' Paul Steadman's tone was shocked. 'Even if he is a suspect, you mustn't suggest it or you'll find yourself being sued for slander and your husband flung out of his job.'

Jane nodded abstractedly. 'If it should turn out to be Richard Corby, surely *you* wouldn't have to do the case, would you, Paul?'

'No, of course not. But at the moment there's no prospect of him or anyone else being charged. That's why you've got to be careful if Linda rings up. Say that your husband never talks shop when he comes home.'

'You don't often, anyway, do you?' she said affectionately.

Steadman sighed, gave her a kiss and set off for whatever the day might bring. It seemed unlikely that there would be any immediate developments.

EIGHTEEN

As Manton drove out of London that morning with Yates, he reflected on the changed nature of their investigation. Originally, when Lucas had been their quarry, it had been a full-blooded game of cops and robbers; now they were stalking an unseen quarry and following a trail which might peter out almost before it had begun.

When they arrived at Blaker's headquarters, Sam Shoe was already there.

'I've told him what it is you wish to see him about', Blaker said brusquely.

'Yes, and you're really asking me something there', the postman broke in, shaking his head dubiously.

'I don't want you to say anything you're not sure about', Manton remarked. 'But I thought you might remember whether you saw Mr. Pringle or Captain Corby when you delivered their mail that morning.'

' 'Course, I quite often do see 'em and then again I quite often doesn't. It all depends, you see.'

'Yes?' Manton asked hopefully.

Sam Shoe looked at him in surprise. 'What I'm trying to tell you, sir, is that it depends on whether they're about or not.'

'I understand that, Mr. Shoe. But do you have any recollection of seeing either of them on the day of the murder?'

The postman rubbed his chin. 'If I says "yes" I

couldn't swear to it, and if I says "no" I couldn't swear to that neither.'

'You just can't remember?'

'Exactly, sir.' His tone implied gratitude to Manton for such a clear understanding of the situation.

'As I warned you', Blaker said, looking across at Manton. 'Anything else you want to ask him before he goes?'

Manton shook his head and Sam Shoe wishing 'good mornings' all round made his exit.

'What do you want to do now?' Blaker asked.

'I think I'll drive over to Five Meadows.'

'Spruille and a couple of my young detective constables are over there making inquiries. I've told them to unearth all the people who might have seen Pringle or Corby between nine and ten that morning—delivery men, any of Pringle's garage customers, etcetera—and have a list ready for you.'

'I imagine their presence will have set the village tongues wagging', Manton observed.

'This morning's papers will have done that already. Much as I should like to think it was Spicer who murdered the old girl—I don't like buggers—I gather we've decided to concentrate on Pringle and Corby.'

'They're our chief interest certainly', Manton agreed.

Half an hour later Yates pulled their car up outside Five Meadows police station. P.C. Green's bicycle was leaning against the side wall and they found the constable himself in the station's office cum inquiry desk.

' 'Morning, Green.'

'Hello, sir. Good morning', Green replied, looking up with a cheerful smile.

'Anything of note to report?'

'Only what's in the papers, sir. That's put the cat properly amongst the pigeons.'

Manton folded his arms and leant comfortably across the counter.

'Tell me what the local rumours are. Who's the village's current favourite for the gallows?'

Green spoke with a faintly deprecating air. 'Mind you, it's only rumour, sir; but most people seem to accept it must have been Bob Pringle who did it.'

'What's the popular theory?'

'Well, they reckon he must have known he was going to benefit under Mrs. Easterberg's will and that he decided to hasten on events.'

'It's certainly a possibility', Manton said thoughtfully.

'And of course there'd have been nothing unusual in his going up to the house. He was always doing so', Green added.

Manton silently studied the frank, open face of the young constable, pondering what he had just said.

'Look, Green, you've been in this village for several years, you must know most of its inhabitants as well as anyone can; who do you think is most likely to have done it?'

Green assumed a thoughtful frown. After a pause he said, 'I don't reckon rumour to be such a lying jade on this occasion, sir.'

'So you also think it was Pringle?'

'Let's say this, sir. I think he had the motive, the know-how and the temperament.'

'What about Corby?'

'Captain Corby's rather a weak character, sir. If he'd murdered his aunt, I'd have expected him to have cracked by now. He hasn't really got the guts to have seen this lot through.'

'Mmm', Manton said, thoughtful in his own turn.

It was at this moment that Sergeant Spruille came in.

'Phew! I'm hot. Hello, sir, I'm sorry I didn't see it was you at first.'

'Learnt anything?'

'Only that most people can be induced to remember almost anything, if you set about asking them the right way. Half the folk I spoke to hadn't an idea at first who or what they'd seen on the morning of the murder. They might have been on another planet for all they remembered, but once their imaginations got going . . . I tell you, sir, Pringle was seen in at least half a dozen widely separated places around half-past nine that morning.'

'Corby, too?'

'I don't know, sir. D.C. Elliot's concentrating on the Corby likelies. I concerned myself only with those who might have seen Pringle.'

'And you learnt nothing on which any reliance could be placed?'

'Nothing, sir. Short of putting heavy weights on Pringle, I don't see that we'll ever squeeze out the truth.'

Manton nodded forlornly. 'It's hopeless expecting anyone to remember something which was of no consequence at the time and which happened nearly eight weeks ago. And yet we're bound to try. It's not until every sterile avenue has been explored that this inquiry can be closed.'

'Have you asked Miss Chatt, sir?' Green asked suddenly, his voice breaking into the atmosphere of gloom which had descended upon them.

'Asked her what?'

'Whether she saw Pringle that morning. I know it was her custom to fill up with petrol at his garage on her way up to London each Wednesday. We know she left the house only shortly before the murder was committed and if by any chance she saw Pringle at the garage, it would more or less rule him out.'

'And if she didn't . . . ' Manton mused aloud.

'If she didn't, sir, then it means he could have been up at the Chase.'

'It's worth investigating, anyway', Manton agreed. 'We'll call on her on our way back to town.' He turned to Yates. 'You've got the address she's staying at?'

'Yes, sir. It's twenty-two Southlea Grove, Harrow.'

'I think someone should also have a word with Gawler. He might remember where his boss was that morning.'

'I'll do that, sir', said Sergeant Spruille. 'Though I doubt whether he'll admit anything which might look bad for Pringle, even supposing he's in a position to.'

A little later, Manton put a call through to the Yard to find out whether any fresh information had come in for him there. He had a team of officers spending the day cross-checking the details of everything Lucas had told the police, as well as pursuing other routine lines of inquiry, but so far nothing had been reported.

Leaving Blaker's officers to continue their inquiries in Five Meadows, he and Yates drove back to London about lunchtime.

They found Southlea Grove after calling at the local police station and ascertaining its whereabouts.

The door of No. 22 was opened by a woman whom Manton had no difficulty in identifying as Miss Chatt's cousin.

'Is Miss Chatt in?'

'No. No, I'm afraid she's not.' The woman seemed flustered. 'I'm expecting her back any moment.'

Manton introduced Yates and himself and the woman at once looked more worried.

'Nothing's happened to Miss Chatt, has it?' she asked.

'Not as far as we're aware. Why, what . . .'

Before he could get any further, the woman blurted out,

'She went out in the middle of the morning and she's never come back. It's now nearly half-past two. I waited lunch for her till half-past one and then I had mine. I can't think where she's gone or what can have happened to her.'

'Did she tell you where she was going?' Manton asked.

'She said she had a little shopping to do and would take a short walk before lunch.'

'What time did she leave?'

'Soon after half-past eleven.'

Manton looked at his watch.

'So she's been gone around three hours', he observed reflectively.

'It's so unlike her not to be back punctually for lunch. I'm frightened she must have been taken ill or knocked down by a car or something.'

'Are you on the telephone?' The woman nodded. 'If I may use it to ring up the local station we'll soon find out whether anything of that sort has been reported.'

Miss Chatt's cousin led them into the front room and indicated the telephone. A few seconds later Manton was through to the police station and speaking to the desk sergeant.

'Funny you should ask that, sir, we've just had a report come through of a woman who was found unconscious on a park bench. She's on her way to hospital now. From a brief description, she sounds as though she might be the person you're asking about.'

Telling Miss Chatt's cousin that they would get in touch with her again shortly, Manton and Yates bounded from the house and into their car.

An ambulance was pulling away from the hospital casualty entrance as they arrived. Down the long corridor inside, they could see a stretcher being borne. They hurried in and caught it up just as an outraged hospital sister tried to bar their way.

On the stretcher, pallid and with features grotesquely sagging, lay Miss Chatt.

NINETEEN

'An overdose of aspirin', the young doctor said laconically, coming into the room where Manton and Yates were waiting.

'Will she live?'

'Unless there are any unforeseen complications, yes.'

'When can we see her?'

'Not yet.'

'When?'

'Depends on the rate of her recovery.'

'Will you bear in mind, doctor, that it's vital for us to talk to her at the earliest possible moment?'

The young doctor gazed at them with an ironical expression.

'You police, you're always wanting people saved from death by their own hand so that you can mete it out to them according to your own rules.'

Manton shrugged impatiently.

'Not our rules, doctor. The laws of the land if you like.'

It was the doctor's turn to shrug. 'It would have saved a lot of public time and expense if this unfortunate woman had died.'

'It's still better we should know why she wanted to.'

'Don't you know already?' the doctor asked, with patent disbelief.

'I can make guesses, but they might be very wide of the mark.'

'Oh, well, it's your problem, not mine.' He sighed resignedly. 'She doesn't look like a murderess.'

'They never do. Moreover, she mayn't be one. But that's what I hope to find out as soon as you'll let me see her.'

'Come back around seven o'clock.'

'All right, but meanwhile I'd like to leave a police-woman at her bedside.'

'If you must.' The doctor smiled wanly and left them.

'We'd better set up a temporary headquarters at the police station here', Manton said, turning to Yates. 'We'll get back there now and phone Blaker and the Yard. Better also let the D.P.P. know.'

Paul Steadman gave a low whistle of surprise as, in a few short sentences, Manton told him what had happened.

'Thanks for ringing', he said. 'I'll tell the Director and expect to hear from you again later.'

From Scotland Yard, Manton learnt that one of his officers had returned and had asked to speak with him when he called. The connection was made.

'Yes, Manton speaking.'

'I got back about half an hour ago, sir. Miss Chatt's hairdresser alibi still holds up, sir. The girl who did her hair is quite definite she kept an appointment that morning. . . .'

'It's not exactly an alibi', Manton broke in. 'But no matter; anything else?'

'No, sir. I was only going to add that the attendant says she knows it was that day because she'd been wondering whether Miss Chatt would have got the card asking her to make it half an hour earlier than had been arranged. The original appointment had been for half-past twelve, but they sent Miss Chatt a card the day before asking if she could come at twelve instead and she did.' He paused and when Manton made no comment went on, 'Wouldn't twelve give her an alibi, sir?'

'No', Manton said vaguely and it was clear that his thoughts were elsewhere. 'No, it wouldn't actually, but, by God, it proves something else.'

Miss Chatt lay back against the mound of pillows which propped her up. She looked pale and infinitely tired.

Manton, Yates and a nurse stood round her bed watching her intently. Her eyes had met Manton's, shown recognition and turned away again to stare unseeingly into the distance.

'Do you feel well enough to answer a few questions, Miss Chatt? The doctor says you're better now', he added, as though to induce her acquiescence. She made no reply and he went on quietly, 'Why did you take all that aspirin?'

Her lips moved slowly and the officers had to strain to catch her words.

'It was the best way.'

'Why was it the best way?'

Again her reply came as a painful whisper. 'Your further inquiries . . . horrible suspicion on everyone . . . bad enough when Lucas charged.'

Manton drew a deep breath.

'Miss Chatt, you don't have to answer my questions unless you wish to, do you understand that?' It wasn't the strict form of caution but it sufficed for the occasion. She nodded her head and for a time her chin remained resting on her chest. Then slowly she looked up again. Manton went on, 'Miss Chatt, you received a card from your hairdresser on the morning of Mrs. Easterberg's death, didn't you? A card changing the time of your appointment.' From her expression, it was clear that she was following him closely, though she did nothing to indicate agreement or otherwise with what he was saying. 'You were in the house when the postman came, weren't you, Miss Chatt, otherwise you wouldn't have known you had to go to your hairdresser at twelve instead of half-past twelve?'

She looked suddenly straight at him.

'That was clever of you . . . silly, too, of me . . . but I'm not sorry.'

'It must have been your footsteps which Lucas heard approaching and which caused him to flee through the window.'

'I heard Mrs. Easterberg call out . . . noises from her bedroom . . . when I got there, she was lying unconscious on the floor . . .'

'And you placed the pillow under her head and turned her face into it?' Manton asked, staring with a fascinated expression at the old, grey lady that Miss Chatt had suddenly become. The silence was palpable as the three of them stood in anxious tension round the bed. Manton's tone was quiet and he could hear his own heart beats as he asked the only remaining question that puzzled him still: that not merely puzzled but gnawed furiously at his curiosity. 'Why did you do it, Miss Chatt?'

She brought a hand slowly up to her dry lips and fingered them. The nurse stepped forward and Manton got ready to thrust her aside. He must know the answer; no hospital rules, no feelings of humanity could deprive him of it now.

'Would you like a sip of water, dear?' the nurse asked, ignoring Manton as he closed to her side.

Miss Chatt shook her head.

'No.'

'Would you like these men to go? Have you had enough?'

'Let her answer my question', Manton hissed fiercely.

'I'll tell you . . . then you can go', Miss Chatt said, closing her eyes and opening them again with a sort of determined physical effort. 'She despised me . . . harassed me . . . and she'd found out I'd been stealing from her . . . had said she'd have to tell Captain Corby, because it was he who had recommended me to her. . . .' Through Manton's mind, there came an immediate recollection of the mysterious telephone call Mrs. Easterberg had made to her nephew.

'Did you hear Mrs. Easterberg speak to Captain Corby on the phone that morning?' he asked urgently.

'Asked him to come and see her . . . I knew it was about me . . . cat and mouse game . . . I wouldn't have killed her, but when I saw her lying on the floor and I thought . . . I thought . . . I thought of everything . . .' Her voice trailed off and her eyes closed in exhaustion.

'You must go now', the nurse said in a worried tone.

'Yes, we'll go', Manton replied, suddenly beginning to ache in every limb. 'We've learnt all we came to learn. We've learnt who murdered Mrs. Easterberg, and why.'

TWENTY

The next morning when Manton phoned the hospital, it was to be informed that Miss Chatt had developed pneumonia; that her condition was serious and aggravated by her lack of will to pull through.

It was then that he knew she would die, and was glad for her, for now that the case was solved he had no wish to take the pound of flesh which the doctor had suggested was his only interest.

Twenty-four hours later Miss Chatt did die, and in the week that followed the case slipped from the headlines, leaving those who had been swept up by its floodtide to readjust their lives.

Before Paul Steadman had time to put away the Lucas file, however, he had been caught up in the affairs of a gelignite gang who had shown considerable skill and industry until one day one of its members was blown up in addition to the bank safe beside which his body was found. It gave promise of being an intriguing case.

It was some three weeks later that Manton had occasion to drive down to Five Meadows to clear up a few loose ends connected with the murder.

As he drove into the village a large removal van parked outside the Corbys' cottage caught his eye. Then he noticed two white-aproned figures staggering down the garden path beneath the weight of a massive wardrobe. Through the open front door he could see Linda Corby directing further operations.

'The Corbys leaving?' he inquired of P.C. Green when, minute or two later, he arrived at the police station.

'Yes, sir.'

'Anyone know why?'

'Oh, yes, sir. There isn't any mystery about it. It's ecause of Bob Pringle. He's made it plain to all that he oesn't intend to move and so the Corbys have got to. At ast, that's Mrs. Corby's reasoning.'

'Did she say so herself?' Manton asked with interest.

Green smiled. 'Came in special to tell me, sir. She asn't going to leave Five Meadows without making sure iat we all knew the reason. She's told everyone that it's uite unthinkable for the Captain and herself to go on ving in the same district as Pringle after what's hapened.'

'And Pringle's remaining here?'

'He's already started enlarging his premises, sir', Green id dryly and Manton gave a short laugh.

A little later, his business completed, he shook hands ith Green and strolled out to his waiting car. He reached ie gate and noticed a familiar figure walking past on the r side of the road.

'Hello, Jean', he called out.

The girl turned at the sound of his voice and, for a cond, studied him gravely. Then she smiled.

'Hello.'

He walked over to her.

'Life treating you well?' She smiled again but said othing and he went on, 'Been seeing anything of ave?'

'We're getting married', she said shyly, and blushed.

Before he could help himself, Manton's eyes had swept own and she blushed further.

'That's fine, Jean', he said guiltily. 'I hope you'll be

very happy.' In a lighthearted tone he added, 'You're taking on a big job.'

Afterwards, as he watched her go off down the street he stood pondering the triteness of his remarks. Big job indeed! It was more than that, a girl of seventeen, marrying, through force of circumstances, a young man with a strong, if not irrevocable, propensity towards crime. Big job! He turned back to his car and shrugged his shoulders in self-disgust and as if to shed a problem which wasn't his by any right.

But as he drove towards London he supposed he would nevertheless have to try and see Lucas: not to talk him out of marriage to Jean, but into a sense of some of the responsibilities this event would bring. It might prove to be so much waste of breath but at least he would have satisfied the dictate of his conscience.

Gazing absently out of the car as the driver wove his way through central London's traffic, he caught a sudden glimpse of the figure of justice, gleaming high above the Old Bailey in the afternoon sun.

It was the first time since the trial that he had consciously observed her and he recalled the disparaging comment he had mouthed up at her after Lucas's acquittal. He now made a little bow of belated acknowledgement. For she had been right after all.

THE END